# THE VENGEANCE RIDERS

# THE VENGEANCE RIDERS

When rancher Tom Hawke of the Diamond H vanishes while riding from Colorado to the Texas Panhandle on a cattle-buying expedition, his son, ex-ranger Jackson Hawke, sets out to solve the mystery of his father's disappearance.

All the evidence suggests that the marshal of Bedlam and his deputy, working under the control of the unscrupulous owner of the nearby Circle B Ranch, Matt Boone, are responsible for Tom Hawke's disappearance and probable murder. But is this really the case?

Can Jackson possibly succeed in the difficult and dangerous task of bringing the criminals to justice?

# The Vengeance Riders

*by*

Alan Irwin

**Dales Large Print Books**
Long Preston, North Yorkshire,
BD23 4ND, England.

British Library Cataloguing in Publication Data.

---

Irwin, Alan
    The vengeance riders.

    A catalogue record of this book is
    available from the British Library

    ISBN   1-84262-233-1 pbk

First published in Great Britain in 2002 by Robert Hale Limited

Copyright © Alan Irwin 2002

Cover illustration © Prieto by arrangement with
Norma Editorial S.A.

Published in Large Print 2003 by arrangement with
Robert Hale Limited

Dales Large Print is an imprint of Library Magna Books Ltd.

Printed and bound in Great Britain by
T.J. (International) Ltd., Cornwall, PL28 8RW

# ONE

It was a warm afternoon. Marshal Hank Tomlin, seated behind the desk in his office on the main street of Bedlam in the northern section of New Mexico Territory, woke from a short nap and rose to stretch his legs. He was a big man, overweight, with small eyes and a heavily jowled face.

He walked over to the window and looked out along the street. It was deserted, save for one rider heading into town. He was a stranger to the marshal, who stood watching him as he rode up to the livery stable, dismounted, and led his horse inside.

The stranger was tall, slim and middle-aged, with a neatly trimmed beard. He was well dressed and was riding a big chestnut gelding with a white stripe down its face. He wore a Texas hat, with a big five-point Texas star on one side, and a bandanna of somewhat flamboyant hue and pattern.

There was a responsible air about the stranger, and Tomlin, wondering what he was doing in town, put him down as a businessman of some sort, or maybe a rancher.

Tomlin's second guess was on target. The man was Tom Hawke, who ran a medium-sized spread, the Diamond H, not far south of Pueblo, in Colorado. The rancher was on his way to the Triple K ranch in the Texas Panhandle to negotiate with the owner Ben Kincaid the purchase and delivery to the Diamond H of a sizeable herd of breeding cattle. Kincaid's expertise in breeding and calf production was well known among the cattle-raising community.

Inside the stable, Hawke handed the chestnut over to the liveryman Clem Brown, a pleasant-looking, grey-haired man in his late fifties.

'I figure on leaving tomorrow morning,' he said.

'Right,' said Brown, eyeing the chestnut. 'That sure is one good-looking animal. I'll feed and water him right away.'

'I ain't been in Bedlam before,' said the rancher. 'I'm wondering how the place comes to have a fancy name like that.'

'The town was founded about eight years ago, when a prospector hit a big pocket of gold nearby,' Brown told him. 'When the word got around about the find, prospectors flooded in, all aiming to make their fortune, and the place was like a madhouse for a while. One of the prospectors called it Bedlam, and the name stuck.

'But the find petered out after a couple of years and soon things quietened down considerable. Nowadays, the main reasons for it being here are the big Circle B ranch in the valley, the stagecoach office, and a few small ranches and homesteads outside the valley.'

After chatting to the liveryman for a short while the rancher walked over to the hotel on the far side of the street and took a room for the night. He lay resting on the bed for a spell, then went down the stairs and through into the small dining-room for a meal.

When he had finished this he left the hotel and walked along the street and into the saloon. Three men were standing at the bar and four others were seated at a table playing poker. Two of the players were wearing lawmen's badges. Hawke walked up to the bar and asked for a beer, then stood at the bar drinking it and looking over at the table where the poker game was in progress.

The two lawmen at the table were Marshal Tomlin, who had watched Hawke ride into town, and his deputy Warren Fisher. Fisher was a short, swarthy man, with a scar showing over his right eyebrow. The other two men were Davis, the agent in charge of the stagecoach office, and Matt Boone, owner of the nearby Circle B ranch. Boone was a big man, in his early fifties, well dressed, and with an arrogant look about him.

As Hawke watched, Davis threw his cards

down and a moment later left the table and walked out of the saloon. Tomlin, who was facing Hawke, called across to him.

'We've got a poker game going here, stranger,' he said. 'You like to sit in?'

Hawke hesitated. He was, in fact, a keen poker-player and a very good one to boot, as his friends would testify. He wasn't particularly tired and he couldn't think of a better way of passing the time till he felt like turning in.

'Sure,' he said, and walked over to the table, taking his drink with him. The marshal introduced himself and his two companions. Hawke gave his name and told the others that he owned a ranch near Pueblo and was riding to the Panhandle to buy some breeding cattle.

The rancher Boone asked Hawke where he was buying his cattle. The bearded Circle B owner was trying hard to give the impression of being a sociable type of individual. 'I'm hoping to get them,' said Hawke, 'from a man called Kincaid who runs the Triple K Ranch in the Panhandle.'

'I've heard of him,' said Boone. 'He has a good reputation for the quality of his cattle. Now let's play some poker.'

Hawke soon discovered that his own poker-playing ability was well above that of the three other men at the table. The best of the three was Boone. The changing expressions on the faces of the two lawmen as the game progressed were keenly observed by Hawke.

Poker-faced, he added to the pot, from time to time, banknotes which he took from a big roll in the pocket of his jacket. Clearly he was carrying a large amount of money on him.

'That's a lot of money you're carrying around, Mr Hawke.' said Boone. 'Ain't you scared somebody might get the idea of taking it away from you by force?'

'I figured I was safe in present company,' said Hawke, 'especially with two lawmen sitting in the game. I sure don't aim to make a habit of flashing it around. I need it to pay for the cattle I'm buying from Kincaid. He's expecting me to turn up at the Triple K in a couple of days.'

As the game progressed the cards ran well for Hawke, and that, as well as his superior skill at the game, produced a substantial pile of winnings on the table in front of him. He decided he was ready to quit and go to his room at the hotel. The others exchanged glances, but raised no objections when he suggested this.

'I'd appreciate a few minutes of your time before you go,' said Boone. 'I'm interested in the area around Pueblo from the cattle-raising point of view. Maybe you could give me some advice.'

'Sure,' said Hawke.

'I'll be back in a minute,' said Boone. 'I'm going over to the bar for a cigar.'

The marshal and his deputy walked across the room with Boone, and the rancher had a brief talk with them before they left the saloon together. Boone bought a cigar from the barkeep and returned to Hawke for a conversation which lasted about fifteen minutes.

'I'll let you go now,' said Boone, 'and thanks for the advice. I'm going to the hotel myself. I'll walk along there with you.'

They left the saloon and walked along the boardwalk towards the hotel, which was on the same side of the street. Boone was between Hawke and the street. They walked along the front of the general store and started to cross the end of an alley between the store and the stagecoach office, both of which were closed. The street was deserted.

Suddenly, Boone turned towards Hawke, pulled the rancher's gun from its holster, and pushed him violently sideways into the alley. The marshal, waiting there for him, grabbed him by the neck. Before Hawke could retaliate effectively the deputy marshal stabbed him twice in the back with a long-bladed knife.

Tomlin released his hold and stepped out of the way as Hawke fell forward against the rough timber wall of the store, with his arms outstretched. Gradually, he slid downwards until he lay crumpled on the ground at the foot of the wall.

Boone stepped out of the alley and looked up and down the street. It was still deserted. He went back to Hawke and removed the thick roll of banknotes from his pocket.

'We'll share these out later,' he said. 'Is he dead?'

'He sure is,' said Fisher. 'I know just where the knife went.'

Boone knelt down and checked Hawke's pulse.

'You're right,' he said. 'It was a stroke of luck for us, a well-heeled stranger coming into the saloon like that. It ain't often the chance comes along to make a pile of money like this so easy. Now we've got to get the body out of town as quick as we can.'

He thought for a moment, then spoke to Fisher.

'Get my horse,' he said. 'It's outside the saloon. Bring it round to the back of the stagecoach office. The marshal and me'll carry the body round there and we'll sling it across the back of the horse. Then you'll ride the horse along the trail towards the ranch until you reach that thick patch of brush three miles from here, by the side of the trail.

'When you reach it, drag the body into the middle of the brush, out of sight, and hightail it back here. We'll be in the marshal's office. We can bury the body somewhere else, later on.'

Ten minutes later, Fisher rode off with the body, and Boone and Tomlin went to the marshal's office. After a brief discussion there, Boone went back to the saloon and walked up to Brown, the liveryman, who was standing at the bar in the same position that he had been occupying when Boone left the saloon with Hawke earlier.

Boone knew that there was still an hour to go before Brown's usual time of departure from the saloon. He engaged the liveryman in conversation for some twenty minutes. He said that he was figuring on buying some quarter horses and he asked Brown if he knew of any places, not too far away, where he could get what he wanted.

While Boone was talking with Brown, the marshal slipped into the stable, saddled Hawke's horse, and led it out of the rear door of the stable, closing the door behind him. Then, after checking that there was nobody out on the street, he led the animal to the rear of his office. He tethered it there and went into the office.

A few minutes later he was joined by Boone. Both men left the office and crossed over the street to the hotel. Boone parted from Tomlin and went inside. He walked up to the hotel owner, Bart Bellamy, who was standing near the desk, and a moment later the marshal, watching from outside, saw the two men disappear from view into a room behind the desk.

Tomlin slipped noiselessly into the hotel, got Hawke's room number from the register, and took his room key from a hook on the wall. Then he walked silently up the stairs, along the passage, and let himself into

Hawke's room. He collected all the dead man's belongings into a sack he had brought with him. Carrying the sack, he left the hotel and returned to his office.

Ten minutes later, Boone joined the marshal in his office and they sat down to await the return of the deputy.

'Nobody needs to know about this business but the three of us and Sadler out at the ranch,' said Boone. 'I'm going to get him to give you a hand getting rid of the body. Our story had better be that I parted from Hawke outside the hotel, then came to this office for a while before I went back to the saloon to talk to Brown. Then I rode back to the ranch.

'You two had better take the body out of the valley as soon as you can. It's just struck me that a good place to bury it would be in the middle of that grove of trees that stands against the northbound trail about six miles out of Bedlam.'

'I know where you mean,' said Tomlin. 'It's a good place to hide a body. And I don't think we should waste any time. I think we should bury him tonight.'

'All right,' said Boone. 'You can start out when Fisher gets back. Take those things you got from Hawke's room and bury them with him. And don't forget his hat. You'll need to take spades and a lamp with you. I'll get Sadler to meet you at the burying place.'

'How about Hawke's horse?' asked Tomlin.

'We can't risk it being found anywhere around here,' said Boone. 'Shoot it and bury it in the same place.'

'It's a pity,' said Tomlin. 'That's a fine animal.'

'Bury it,' said Boone, 'We want it to look like Hawke, after the poker game, decided for some reason that he didn't want to stay in town overnight, and got his horse from the stable and rode off.'

Some time later, when Fisher returned on Boone's horse, the rancher rode off on his way to the Circle B. Thirty minutes later, just after midnight, the marshal and his deputy left to pick up Hawke's body. Fisher was leading Hawke's horse. With the help of Sadler, who was waiting for them at the grove, they buried the bodies of Hawke and his horse. Then, before daylight, the lawmen returned to Bedlam, and Sadler rode back to the Circle B.

Later in the morning, both the hotel owner and the liveryman reported to the marshal that Hawke appeared to have ridden off in the night without settling his bills.

# TWO

Just over ninety miles north of Bedlam, on the Diamond H ranch near Pueblo, at the time that Tom Hawke was starting the poker game with Boone and the others, Tom's son Jackson was riding up to the ranch house. On the previous day, his mother Mary Hawke had received a telegraph message from him letting her know that he would be turning up at the ranch shortly. Jackson, just over thirty years old, clean-shaven and dark-haired, was a well-built man a little under six feet tall, with a self-confident look about him. He had tried his hand at prospecting and driving a stagecoach on the overland route. Most recently, over the past three years, during which he had not seen his parents, he had been serving as a ranger in Texas. Now he was figuring to look around for a lawman's job in Colorado.

'That's good news, Jackson,' his mother said, when he told her this. 'You'll be able to stay with me till your father gets back? He reckoned he'd be away maybe eight days. He said he'd telegraph me when he'd clinched a deal with Kincaid on the Triple K.'

'Sure I'll stay,' said Jackson, 'and I'll hang on here for a while after father gets back. I ain't in no hurry to leave.'

Looking out of the ranch house window,

Jackson saw the ramrod Pete Harley riding in from the range. Harley had worked on the Diamond H for the past six years and Jackson knew him well. He was aware that there was complete trust between the ramrod and his parents. He went out to have a talk with Harley.

The ramrod was obviously pleased to see him. Jackson told him of his own plans, then asked Harley how things were going on the ranch.

'Pretty well,' said the ramrod. 'We're building up a quality herd and there's a good market for the beef we have to sell.'

Jackson chatted with Harley for a while, then went with him to meet the other hands, several of whom he knew. Then he returned to the ranch house.

Four days later, in the evening, he was discussing with his mother the fact that no message had yet been received from his father about his progress on the cattle deal.

'I was sure,' she said, 'that we'd have heard from him by now. He was due to reach the

Triple K a couple of days ago. He promised to send me a telegraph message when he arrived.'

'Maybe that message got held up for some reason,' said Jackson. 'Maybe the telegraph line is down. But if we don't hear anything by tomorrow noon I'll ride into Pueblo and send a message to Kincaid at the Triple K asking him whether father's turned up there.'

No message arrived in the morning, and in the afternoon Jackson rode to Pueblo and went inside the telegraph office. The operator confirmed that no message for his mother had yet been received. Jackson wrote out a message for Kincaid at the Triple K, asking whether his father had arrived there. He handed the message to the operator, then returned to the ranch to await the reply.

It came in the afternoon two days later, brought from Pueblo by one of the ranch hands. It read: *Mr Hawke expected here but no sign of him yet. Will telegraph you if he turns up. Kincaid.*

'I'm worried, Jackson,' said Mary Hawke. 'That was a long ride your father set out on. Something's happened to him on the way.'

'It sure looks like he's got held up somewhere,' said Jackson. 'I'm going to ride after him right now. Have you any notion of the route he was taking?'

'He was going to camp out the first night,' she said, 'and on the second night he was aiming to stay at a town called Bedlam that somebody told him about. It's just over the New Mexico border. After that I think he was going to ride south-east through New Mexico Territory and across the border into the Panhandle.'

Jackson got a description from his mother of the clothes his father was wearing when he left the Diamond H. Then he went to see Harley, the ramrod, to tell him of Tom Hawke's non-appearance at the Triple K.

Riding off soon after dark, Jackson left a worried woman behind him. He had promised to send her a message immediately he had any firm news about her husband.

He headed straight for Bedlam, hoping to get news of his father there. He took a couple of hours' rest on the trail before dawn, and rode into Bedlam during the afternoon of the day following his departure. His first call was at the livery stable. He dismounted and walked inside. Clem Brown, tending to a horse at the back of the stable, stopped what he was doing and walked over to Jackson.

'Howdy,' he said.

'Howdy,' replied Jackson. 'Maybe you can help me. I think my father probably called in here about eight days ago on his way to the Texas Panhandle. Trouble is, he ain't arrived at the place he was heading for and my mother and me, we're worried about what might've happened to him.

'His name's Tom Hawke. He's a tall man, slim and bearded. He was riding a big chestnut gelding with a white stripe on its face. D'you recollect seeing him here in town? Maybe he left the chestnut with you?'

'He sure did,' said the liveryman. 'It was eight days ago, like you said. He brought the horse in and said he was going to stay overnight. But he rode out between ten and eleven in the evening, while I was in the saloon. And he plumb forgot to leave anything to cover the stabling of the horse.'

'That don't sound like my father,' said Jackson, 'and I can't account for it. But anything he owes you, I'll pay. Did he look all right to you?'

'Sure,' Brown replied. 'He spent the evening in the saloon, playing poker, and came out well on top. When he left the saloon, that was the last I saw of him. When I got back to the livery stable later, I noticed his horse was gone.

'The following morning, I checked with Bart Bellamy who owns the hotel here, and we went up to the room your father had been using. It was empty. All his things were gone. And he hadn't paid his hotel bill.'

'I'll settle that, too,' said Jackson. 'Who

were the other players in that poker game?'

'They were Matt Boone, who owns the big Circle B Ranch in the valley,' said Brown, 'and Marshal Hank Tomlin and his deputy, Warren Fisher.'

Jackson paid the money owed by his father and asked Brown to look after his horse. Then he walked across the street to the hotel and stood outside it for a while, digesting the information he had just received from the liveryman.

He was deeply worried. In the first case, it was inconceivable to him that his father would ride off leaving unpaid bills behind; secondly, he knew that his father, whose night vision was poor, was strongly averse to riding alone in the dark.

He went to the stagecoach office and asked Davis the station agent what was the best way for him to get a message to his mother at the Diamond H Ranch near Pueblo.

'Give it to me,' said Davis, 'and I'll make sure it's handed in at the nearest telegraph office. Any reply can be addressed to my office here.'

'Thanks,' said Jackson, and wrote a message for his mother saying he was staying on in Bedlam for a while and asking her to let him know, care of the stagecoach office, if she got any news of his father.

His next call was at the hotel. The owner Bellamy, was standing near the desk. Jackson asked him for a room. 'I'm giving you Room 2,' said Bellamy. 'It's one of my best.' Then he stopped, and reconsidered.

'Sorry,' he said. 'I'd forgotten. Room 2's got a damaged bed, and a door lock that needs changing. It won't be ready for a few days. Room 3'll have to do.'

He handed the key over, and Jackson signed the register. As he was doing this he saw his father's signature on the previous page. He pointed to this, and spoke to Bellamy.

'This man,' he said, 'is my father. He's gone missing and I'm looking for him. I heard he'd left owing you money, which ain't like him at all. Put it on my bill.'

'I was plumb surprised,' said Bellamy, 'to find that he'd left in the night like that, after he'd told me he wouldn't be leaving till morning.'

'Did you see him come into the hotel after he'd finished playing poker in the saloon?' asked Jackson.

'No, I didn't,' Bellamy replied, 'but I was busy in the dining-room that evening. I could easily have missed seeing him come in.'

Jackson went up to his room and sat down on the bed. He was becoming increasingly apprehensive about the situation. He was certain that his father would never have ridden off during the night of his own accord. He had either been taken away by force and was being held somewhere, or he had been killed and his body had been disposed of.

He decided that, on the following day, he would find out as much about his father's movements in Bedlam as possible.

He slept only fitfully that night, and, after breakfast in the hotel, he walked along to the livery stable. He spoke to Brown, who was standing outside.

'I'm right, am I,' he asked, 'when I say that nobody saw my father actually ride out of town?'

'That's correct, as far as I know,' replied the liveryman. 'Leastways, nobody's claimed to have seen him, and everybody in town knows about him disappearing like he did.'

'You said you were in the saloon when he left,' said Jackson. 'Did he leave alone?'

'No,' replied Brown, 'Boone was with him. The marshal and his deputy had left a little earlier. Boone came back to the saloon a bit later. He wanted some advice from me about where he might buy some quarter horses. He stayed with me about twenty minutes, then he left.'

'Looks like I'd better have a talk with Boone then, as well as with the marshal,' said Jackson. 'Where will I find the Circle B ranch house?'

'Follow the trail leading east out of town for six miles,' said Brown, 'and you'll see the ranch buildings in the middle of the valley. If you want to see the marshal, you'll have to wait a while. I saw him riding out of town with his deputy a couple of hours ago. I don't know where they were going.'

'Thanks,' said Jackson. 'I'll be back for my horse in fifteen minutes.'

As he was about to leave Brown, his eye was caught by a man on the boardwalk outside the saloon on the far side of the street. He was cleaning the boardwalk, using a stiff broom and a large bucket of water. He was working spasmodically, pausing from time to time to stare into space for a while, then restarting with renewed vigour. He waved to Brown, and the liveryman responded.

'That's my elder brother Will,' he told Jackson, sadly. 'He's only half a man, I guess. Ten years ago he was captured and tortured by Comanches. He was rescued by the Army, but not before he'd turned half

31

crazy. The saloon-keeper's a good friend of ours. Will does a few odd jobs for him around the saloon. And he helps me out in the stable as well.'

'D'you reckon he might have seen my father pick up his horse at the stable on the night he disappeared?' asked Jackson.

'No,' replied Brown. 'We both sleep in the house behind the stable, and I know that Will always turns in well before the time your father left the saloon.'

He turned to look at a horse coming into town from the east. Its rider was a burly man, bearded and hawk-nosed. He wore a right-hand gun.

'That's Barclay,' he said, 'one of Boone's men. He ain't been here long, but the word is he's a quarrelsome man with a short temper and a pretty high opinion of himself as a gunslinger. I could never see the sense in Boone employing a man like him. And the same goes for most of the other hands in Boone's outfit. They ain't a bit like the cowhands I met up with in Texas before I moved up here.'

He looked along the street towards the sound of children's voices. A group of young boys had run out from behind the saloon and were playing tag in the street.

As Jackson started walking towards the store to make some purchases, Barclay dismounted outside the saloon and tied his horse to a hitching rail. He stood near the edge of the boardwalk for a moment, rolling a cigarette.

Will Brown, still working on the boardwalk, stumbled backwards as two running boys brushed past him, and knocked the almost full bucket of water over. Its contents spilled out, soaking the bottom half of Barclay's pants and his boots.

The Circle B hand's face reddened with anger as he stared down at his legs and feet. He jumped up on to the boardwalk. 'You clumsy fool!' he shouted, and struck Will Brown savagely on the side of the face with the back of his hand. His victim staggered sideways, fell off the boardwalk, and ended up lying on his back on the street. Barclay, still incensed, jumped down after him and drew back his right foot with the clear intention of kicking Will Brown in the side. Jackson, who was crossing the street diagonally, saw the incident clearly, and he was about seven yards away from the Circle B hand when Barclay signalled his intention of kicking the man lying on the ground. Jackson drew his Peacemaker and fired a shot which grazed the calf of Barclay's left leg.

Barclay yelled out in pain and dropped his right foot to the ground before the kick had been delivered. He turned to face Jackson, his hand reaching for the handle of his revolver. But the look on Jackson's face and the sight of the gun in his hand persuaded Barclay that drawing his own gun wasn't such a good idea. He stood staring at Jackson, while Clem Brown ran up to help his brother to his feet and lead him off towards the stable.

Half-way there, they stopped and looked

back at Jackson and Barclay. A small group of onlookers, including the boys who had triggered the confrontation, had collected to view the proceedings.

'What a bad-tempered bully you are, Barclay,' said Jackson, as he holstered the Peacemaker. 'You ain't fit to be around other people. In fact, I reckon it'd be a good idea for you to ride out of town and stay out. You ought to be glad I didn't put a bullet through that leg of yours, instead of just nicking it.'

Barclay, rage boiling up inside him, started to turn as if he was intending to limp off towards his horse. Then, confident in his own gun-handling ability, and hoping to catch his opponent unawares, he suddenly twisted back, drawing his gun as he did so.

Jackson, half-expecting the move, made a quick, smooth draw which impressed the onlookers and was too fast for his opponent. The bullet from his Colt smashed into Barclay's chest before the Circle B hand had succeeded in triggering his own gun. He staggered backwards and collapsed on the ground. Jackson walked up and bent over him. He was sure that his bullet had entered the heart, and that Barclay was dead.

Marshal Tomlin, riding into town from the east with his deputy, saw the small group standing on the street. They rode up, dismounted, and pushed through the onlookers until they reached the body. They both recognized the dead man. They looked at Jackson, who was standing close to the body.

'What's happened here?' asked Tomlin.

'I can tell you that,' said Clem Brown, who had walked back with his brother to join the onlookers. 'Barclay started beating up my brother, when Will accidentally spilled some water over his legs.'

He went on to give the marshal details of how Jackson had intervened and had been forced to shoot Barclay.

'It was a clear case of self-defence on Mr Hawke's part,' he said. 'Everybody here will tell you that.'

The marshal grunted. The name 'Hawke' rang a warning bell in his mind. Then he noticed the resemblance between the stranger who had shot Barclay and the rancher he and the others had killed after the poker game in the saloon nine days earlier. He spoke to Jackson.

'You got business in town?' he asked.

'I'm looking for my father, Tom Hawke,' said Jackson. 'I heard that you and your deputy and a rancher called Boone had a game of poker with him nine days ago. Since then, he's gone missing, and Boone was maybe the last man to see him before he disappeared. I aim to see Boone. Maybe my father said something to him before they parted company. Something that might help me to find him.'

'I remember that game,' said the marshal. 'Your father did pretty well out of it. If I recollect right, he left town during the night.

'I'll speak with you about your father later. Just now, I've got to talk with some of the people who saw what happened between you and Barclay. And I've got to get somebody to pick up the body. Don't leave town.'

'I'll be at the livery stable when you want to see me,' said Jackson.

The marshal moved away with his deputy and Jackson moved towards the livery stable with Clem Brown and his brother.

'Ride out to the Circle B,' said Tomlin to Fisher, 'and tell Boone that Hawke's son has turned up in town looking for his father. Tell him that Hawke had a shoot-out with Barclay, and Barclay's dead. And say that Hawke will likely be riding out to the ranch to see him. I'll tend to things here while you're away.'

A few minutes later, the deputy rode out of town.

The marshal talked with several of the onlookers, all of whom gave their opinion that Barclay was entirely responsible for his own demise, the fatal shot from Jackson being fired in self-defence.

At the livery stable, Clem Brown thanked

Jackson for his intervention when Will Brown was under attack. Will had earlier been taken into the house by his brother, who had then returned to Jackson in the stable.

'How is he?' asked Jackson.

'He'll be all right,' said the liveryman. 'He's just shook up a bit. But I reckon he'd be suffering a lot more if you hadn't taken a hand. That Barclay was a violent man, with a very short temper.'

'I'm glad I was around to help,' said Jackson.

'I think,' said Brown, 'that maybe you'd be wise to leave town as soon as the marshal says you can go. I don't know how Boone's going to take this killing. Maybe he'll be after revenge. Maybe he'll send his men after you.'

'I ain't leaving,' said Jackson. 'I've got a strong hunch something happened to my father around here. I've got to find out what that something was.'

When the marshal had arranged for the

body to be picked up by the undertaker he walked over to the livery stable to talk with Jackson.

'It seems,' he said, 'that Barclay got what was coming to him. But all the same, let me warn you, I ain't going to stand for any more gunplay on the streets of Bedlam. I've sent a deputy out to the Circle B to tell Boone about the shooting. He ain't going to be pleased about losing one of his hands. I'd feel a lot better if you left town.'

'I can't do that,' said Jackson. 'Like I told you, my father's gone missing. I was hoping maybe you could help me to find him.'

'I doubt it,' said Tomlin. 'The last that me and my deputy saw of him was when we left him in the saloon. And the next day we heard that his horse was gone and his room was empty. It looks like he rode off in the night without telling anybody.'

'But I happen to know he wouldn't do that,' said Jackson. 'He never rode alone in the dark, especially on trails he hadn't been on before.'

'Well, he sure ain't in town,' said the marshal. 'I've checked that. And that being so, there ain't nothing else I can do for you.'

'In that case, I'll do some nosing around myself,' said Jackson.

Tomlin scowled. 'Just remember what I told you about no more gunplay in town,' he said.

He turned, and walked off in the direction of his office. Jackson turned to the liveryman.

'There's a man I sure can't take to,' he said. 'How come he came to be marshal?'

'He weren't appointed in the ordinary way,' said Brown. 'He was put in the job by Boone, and Boone pays him and Fisher. Most folks in town think it's a bad arrangement.'

'I agree with them,' said Jackson. 'A town marshal should only be appointed by a mayor and council.'

'You going to see Boone?' Brown asked.

'Right after I've had a meal at the hotel,' Jackson replied. 'Does he have any family

41

out there?'

'Only a stepdaughter,' replied Brown. 'His wife died about two years ago.'

## THREE

Jackson rode out of town at one o'clock in the afternoon along the trail heading eastward towards the Circle B. He was almost half-way there when he spotted a horse standing near the trail ahead, with its rider standing close by.

As he rode up to them he saw that the rider was a slim young woman, probably in her early twenties. She was strikingly beautiful, with long raven hair, and large dark eyes set in an oval face. Jackson could see that the horse, a handsome dun, appeared to have a lame left forefoot.

'Howdy, miss,' he said. 'You in trouble?'

'It's my horse Sandy here,' she replied. 'I

was on my way into town from the Circle B and she's just gone lame on me.'

Jackson guessed that the woman was Boone's stepdaughter. He dismounted and took a close look at the left forefoot of the dun.

'It's a bruised sole,' he said. 'The horse must have trod on something pretty sharp. That foot's got to be rested. You ain't going to be able to ride the horse just now. You can ride behind me if you like, and we'll lead the mare to the ranch.'

'I'm Rachel Marsh,' she said. 'My step-father owns the Circle B. I accept that offer of a ride.'

'Jackson Hawke,' said Jackson. 'I was on my way to see your stepfather.'

He helped her on to his horse and handed her the reins of the dun. Then he mounted in front of her and they headed for the ranch.

While they were riding he learnt that she had been living with relatives back East since her mother had died on the Circle B over two years ago. Three months had passed since her return to the ranch.

'Are you enjoying life on the ranch?' asked Jackson.

'Frankly, no,' she replied. 'Mother's not there now, of course, and I only came back because my stepfather insisted. I don't feel comfortable here, and sometimes...' She broke off, then continued: 'But I didn't mean to bother you with my problems.' She fell silent and Jackson told her about his father's disappearance while in Bedlam, and of his own efforts, so far unsuccessful, to find him.

When they arrived at the ranch house, Boone, who had seen them coming, was waiting outside. From the description given him by Deputy Fisher, the rancher was fairly sure that the man with his stepdaughter was Jackson Hawke. The girl dismounted, then Jackson did the same.

'This is Mr Hawke, father,' said Rachel, and went on to explain how her horse had gone lame and how Jackson had helped her get back to the ranch house.

Sadler, the ranch hand who had helped Marshal Tomlin and his deputy to bury Tom Hawke, was standing nearby. Boone shouted to him to come over and take the lame horse away. Then he spoke to Jackson. 'Thank you for helping Rachel out.' he said. 'I reckon you must be the man who shot my hand Barclay, this morning.'

Shocked, Rachel stared at Jackson.

'That's right,' Jackson replied. 'I didn't have any choice. I'm sorry it had to be like that.'

'I can't say I'm pleased,' said the rancher, 'but I got the full story from Deputy Fisher and it looks like Barclay was well in the wrong. I've warned him many a time about that temper of his. I told him it would get him into real trouble one day.'

'I came out here to see you,' said Jackson, 'because I'm looking for my father and maybe you can help me.'

He told Boone about his father's non-arrival at his destination, after apparently leaving Bedlam.

'I heard in town,' said Jackson, 'that my father left the saloon with you after the poker game finished. Can you tell me where you parted company?'

'Sure,' replied Boone. 'He said he was going to the hotel, so I said I'd walk along there with him. When we reached it we chatted outside for a minute or two while I congratulated him on his skill as a poker player. Then he went into the hotel, and I never saw him again.

'I went back to the saloon after I'd had a talk with the marshal in his office, because I remembered I wanted to ask Brown where I could get some good quarter horses. Then I rode back to the ranch.'

'I know for sure that my father wouldn't have ridden off in the night,' said Jackson. 'I think something must have happened to him in Bedlam.'

'That's pretty hard to believe,' said Boone. 'We're a pretty law-abiding lot around here. But if there's anything I or the marshal can do to help, just let us know.'

'Thanks,' said Jackson. 'I'll be leaving now.'

They watched him as he rode off towards town. There was a frown on Boone's face. Rachel asked her father to tell her about the encounter between Jackson and Barclay, and he repeated to her the account he had received from the deputy marshal.

As he rode back to town, Jackson's thoughts kept returning to Rachel Boone, to whom he felt strongly attracted, even though their acquaintance had been so short. Back in town, he went to his room at the hotel and lay on the bed, his mind on the problem of discovering what had happened to his father.

He still felt certain that Tom Hawke would not have ridden away from Bedlam during the night of his own accord. He must, therefore, have been either forcibly abducted, or murdered in town and his body disposed of. Could the motive have been robbery? Jackson knew from his mother that his father was carrying a big roll of banknotes to pay for the cattle he was intending to buy. He decided to continue his enquiries around town the following morning.

When, after a restless night, he was half-way through breakfast, the liveryman came into the dining-room and asked Jackson to call in at the livery stable when he had finished the meal. Jackson agreed, curious about the look of concern on Brown's face.

On his way to the stable he saw Will Brown sweeping the boardwalk outside the saloon. Will gave him a hesitant wave, and Jackson responded. He found Clem Brown inside the stable.

'You remember,' said Brown, 'that you asked me whether Will might have seen your father come into the stable for his horse on the night he disappeared. And I said that he was bound to be in bed at the time?'

'I remember,' said Jackson.

'Well,' said Brown, 'I thought I'd better make sure, so I had a talk with Will this morning. It ain't that easy to hold a conversation with him because his memory comes and goes. But I'm pretty sure now that he did see something that night that you'd want to know about.

'He says he heard a noise outside the house, and looked out of his bedroom window. He saw somebody bring a horse out of the back door of the stable and lead it towards the back of the marshal's office.

'There was enough light coming from that big lamp hanging on the stable wall for him to be pretty sure that the horse was your father's chestnut and that the man leading it was Marshal Tomlin.'

Brown had Jackson's full attention.

'What's your own opinion?' asked Jackson. 'D'you think your brother's right?'

'I do,' said the liveryman. 'There's nothing wrong with Will's eyesight. And he reckons he caught sight of the marshal's badge.'

Jackson pondered for a moment before speaking again. 'What's your opinion of the marshal?' he asked Brown.

'Nobody likes him around here,' Brown replied. 'It's too obvious that he's Boone's man, and that Boone's interests are the main ones that he's looking after.'

'So if the marshal had something to do with my father's disappearance, then Boone may have been involved as well?' said Jackson.

'I reckon that could be so,' Brown replied.

'I'm going to have a look round,' said Jackson. 'Maybe I'll come across some clues outside.'

He left the livery stable, walked over to the saloon, and stood outside the swing doors, looking along the street towards the hotel. He started walking slowly towards the hotel along the path his father must have followed on the night of his disappearance.

He studied the boardwalk as he moved along and when he reached the mouth of the alley between the saloon and the store he walked along it, carefully studying the ground and the wall on either side.

Seeing nothing of interest, he returned to

the street, walked along the boardwalk past the front of the store, then into the alley between the store and the stagecoach office. A few feet along, his eye was caught by a faint brown stain on the ground at the foot of the side wall of the stagecoach office.

Then, from the timber wall, above the stain, hanging from a protruding nail, he spotted a small piece of black material. He removed it and put it in his pocket. He walked slowly down the alley, but could see nothing else of interest.

He walked back into the street, and as he emerged from the alley he saw the marshal watching him through a window in his office on the opposite side of the street. He completed his walk to the hotel, checking the alley between the stagecoach office and the hotel as he did so.

He went to his room in the hotel, took the piece of black material from his pocket and examined it closely. His heart sank. He was almost sure that an expensive jacket bought some time ago by his father was made of the same distinctive material. And according to his mother, his father had been wearing this jacket when he left for the Panhandle.

He reviewed the facts. In his opinion, there was a very strong possibility that his father had been attacked in the alley after leaving the saloon, and was now dead. His father's horse had been spirited away by the marshal. The marshal was probably in cahoots with Boone.

It was difficult for Jackson to figure out just what he should do next, not having any clear proof, only theories, of what lay behind his father's disappearance. He went down for a meal, then spent the afternoon enquiring around town whether anybody, other than Boone, had seen his father after he left the saloon. No one had.

He looked inside a couple of abandoned shacks, then returned to the hotel for supper. Clem Brown was just ordering a meal and he invited Jackson to join him. They were served by a young Mexican woman, Carmen Alvaro, slim and good looking, with dark eyes and jet-black hair.

Brown introduced Jackson to Carmen, and when she went into the kitchen he told Jackson that she was the widow of a Mexican, Juan Alvaro, who had worked for him in his livery stable in South Texas, and had agreed to go with him when Brown decided to move north to Bedlam.

Brown went on to tell Jackson that Juan had died during a cholera epidemic that hit Bedlam two years earlier, and Carmen had stayed on in the small shack behind the stagecoach office. She had refused Brown's offer of money to help her out, and was supporting herself by working in the hotel.

'It ain't much of a life for her, living alone,' said Brown, 'and I've been a mite worried about her lately. There's a Circle B hand who's been pestering her. She's told him she wants nothing to do with him, but he just won't let her be. He's a big red-haired man called Wilson, who fancies himself as a lady-killer. I spoke to the marshal about it, and he said he'd have a word with Wilson. I don't know whether he did or not.'

After supper Jackson stayed in the dining-room for a while, chatting to Bellamy, then went upstairs and into Room 3. A little later, he went into Room 2 next door and took a pile of bedding from the wardrobe. He carried this back to his own room and rolled it into an elongated bundle which he placed under the blanket on his bed to give the appearance that the bed was occupied.

Looking out of his window, he confirmed that there was no balcony outside Rooms 2 and 3. Then he left his room in darkness, locking the door behind him, and re-entered Room 3. He closed the door behind him and sat on a chair in a corner of the room, fully clothed, and wearing his gunbelt.

He sat dozing, getting up occasionally to stretch his legs. At different times between eleven and twelve he heard three separate guests walk along the passage outside, and go into their rooms. Midnight passed, then one o'clock. At about ten minutes after one he thought he heard a slight sound in the passage outside. He rose, walked up to the door, and stood there listening. Suddenly, he heard a crash as the flimsy door of Room 2 was smashed open. This was followed immediately by the sound of four gunshots in rapid succession, then came the sound of someone running along the passage.

Jackson yanked open the door in front of him and peered out into the passage. He saw a man disappearing round the corner at the top of the stairs and took a snap shot at him, hitting him in the arm. Then he went back into the room and looked out of the window, knowing that there was no rear exit from the hotel.

He saw a man run out of the hotel and disappear into the alley between the marshal's office and the livery stable. The build of the man looked identical with that of Fisher, the deputy marshal. Jackson was sure it was him.

The sound of gunfire had roused Bellamy and the other guests. Jackson showed them the bullet-ridden bedding in his room and explained to the hotel-keeper that a strong hunch of danger had persuaded him to keep watch, in Room 3, in case his own room had a visitor during the night.

'Looks like your hunch was right,' said Bellamy. 'I'm going for the marshal right now. And later on, you'd better move your things into Room 5, while we clear this mess up.'

When Tomlin arrived, Jackson told him what had happened, and the marshal examined the bedding and the smashed door. 'Trouble sure seems to hang around you, Hawke,' he said. 'This was a quiet town till you came along. Did you recognize the man who was aiming to kill you?'

'No, I didn't,' lied Jackson. 'I just caught a glimpse of him as he was turning the corner at the top of the stairs. But I had time to put a bullet in his right arm.'

'You sure?' asked the marshal.

'I'm sure,' Jackson replied. 'All you have to do now is find a man with a bullet wound in the right arm, and likely you've got the culprit.'

The marshal looked at him sourly.

'It seems to me,' he said, 'that somebody must have trailed you here with the idea of killing you. I reckon all of us around here would be happier if you moved on.'

'I can't do that,' said Jackson, 'till I know what's happened to my father. I've got a strong feeling he was killed and buried somewhere around here.'

'I ain't found no proof of that,' said Tomlin. 'You stay on here much longer and I'm going to have to run you out of town. You're making a nuisance of yourself, asking questions around the place that there ain't no answers to.'

Glowering at Jackson, he left the room, and shortly afterwards, looking through his room window, Jackson saw him disappear into the alley which the wounded Fisher had entered after leaving the hotel.

Tomlin walked through the alley, then over to the small shack, twenty yards behind the marshal's office, which Fisher was using as living quarters. He could see that there was a light on inside.

He tapped on the door and called out his name. Fisher let him in and closed the door behind him. The deputy's vest and shirt were off and he was obviously in the process of bathing a severe laceration on the upper part of his right arm.

'I put four bullets into Hawke,' he said. 'He's finished, for sure. But somebody shot me in the arm as I was leaving. I can't figure out who it could be.'

'It was Hawke,' said the marshal. 'He rigged the bed to make it look like he was sleeping on it. Then he waited for you in the room next door. He knows he hit you, but he didn't recognize you.'

'Damnation!' said Fisher. 'I was sure I'd got him.'

Tomlin inspected the wound on Fisher's arm.

'You're lucky,' he said, 'that the bullet didn't lodge in there. But it's made a mess of that arm all the same. You ain't going to be able to use it for a while.

'If you stay in town, folks are bound to notice it and put two and two together. You'd better ride out to the Circle B before dawn and ask Boone if you can stay there till it's healed up a bit. He told me once that his cook is pretty good at doctoring. I'll put a bandage on it to get you there. And I'll make up some story for the folks here about sending you out of town yesterday evening on some official business.'

'I'll do what you say,' said Fisher, 'but I ain't looking forward to seeing Boone. He ain't going to be pleased to hear that Hawke's still alive.'

Fisher rode off unseen, an hour before dawn, and Tomlin spent the night on a bunk, provided for occasional use, in his office.

After Tomlin's departure, Jackson moved into Room 5 and lay on the bed, thinking. He was now convinced that both the marshal and his deputy were involved in his father's disappearance, and possible murder. But he did not yet know whether Boone was involved.

He decided that all he could do was to stay on in Bedlam in the hope that eventually he would be able to solve the mystery of his missing father. Meanwhile, he would conceal from the marshal and his deputy the fact that he was certain they were both involved.

## FOUR

When morning came, Jackson went down to the dining-room for breakfast. He was served by the same young Mexican woman, Carmen Alvaro, who had previously been introduced to him by Clem Brown, and he exchanged a few words with her.

After breakfast, he walked to the general store to make a few purchases. The door opened as he approached and Rachel Marsh stepped out. They both stopped and she spoke to him. He sensed that she was still worried about something.

'I'm afraid,' she said, 'that I didn't thank you properly for helping me out the other day, but I was shocked when I heard that you'd shot one of my stepfather's men. I know now that you had no choice in the matter.'

'That's right,' said Jackson. 'I wouldn't like you to have the idea that I get any satisfaction out of killing a man.'

'My stepfather asked me to give you a message,' she said. 'He's heard something which might help you to find out what happened to your father. He's expecting to get more information later today, and he suggests you ride out to the Circle B tomorrow around ten in the morning so's he can pass it all on to you. Can you do that?'

'I'll be there,' said Jackson.

'I don't know what my stepfather's found out,' said Rachel, 'but I hope it'll help.'

'Me too,' said Jackson. 'Will I see you at the ranch tomorrow?'

'I expect so,' she said.

'I've got a feeling there's some sort of problem troubling you,' said Jackson. 'Maybe if you told me about it, I could help you.'

'Thank you,' she said. 'If things get too bad I'll get in touch with you. Maybe you could help.'

She turned abruptly, and walked off towards her horse. After he had made his purchases in the store, Jackson went to see Clem Brown at the livery stable. He asked him if he had seen Deputy Fisher around that morning.

'He ain't in town,' replied Brown. 'I heard that the marshal sent him off yesterday evening on some official business.'

Jackson told Brown that Fisher was the intruder he had shot in the hotel the previous evening, which accounted for his absence from town.

'He's hiding somewhere till that wound heals up,' said Jackson.

'So now you can be sure,' said Brown, 'that both the marshal and his deputy had a hand in your father's disappearance. But what about Boone?'

'I've got no proof yet that he had anything to do with it,' replied Jackson, 'and for the time being I'm not saying anything to anybody but you about Tomlin and Fisher being involved.

'Tomorrow, I'm riding out to the Circle B to see Boone, at his invitation. His step-daughter just told me that he reckons he has information that might help me to find out what happened to my father. Just in case he is involved, I'll keep my eyes peeled for trouble.'

'That's a good idea,' said the liveryman.

As he was leaving the stable Jackson saw a man ride up to the saloon, dismount, and disappear inside. He was a big man with reddish hair, and wearing a gun. He was a stranger to Jackson.

Jackson walked over to the stagecoach office and handed a message for his mother to Davis, the agent. In it, he told her that he still had no news of his father, and that he was staying on in Bedlam because he thought something had happened to his father there.

He chatted with Davis for a while, before leaving and turning into the alley between the general store and the stagecoach office. Once again, he studied the stain on the ground at the point where he was sure his father had been attacked. Then he walked slowly along the alley, examining it closely for any clues he might have missed before. But he was disappointed.

As he reached the end of the alley, and was just about to turn and walk back to the street, his eye was caught by a movement outside the shack occupied by Carmen Alvaro. A man with red hair was standing outside her door. He was the same man that Jackson had seen going into the saloon recently, and Jackson guessed that he was the Circle B hand, Wilson, who had been harassing Carmen.

He saw the man tap on the door, and a moment later it opened. Then, almost immediately, it was slammed shut, but not before Jackson had caught a brief glimpse of Carmen. Wilson knocked again, harder this time. When there was no response, he pushed hard on the door, but it had been fastened inside.

He stepped back a few paces, then launched himself at the flimsy door, striking it with his shoulder. It burst open, and Wilson disappeared inside. A moment later, Jackson heard a woman scream. The scream was cut short, then there was silence.

Jackson was already sprinting over to the shack. He entered it silently.

Wilson, his back to the door, had his hand over Carmen's mouth, and was forcing her down on to the bed at the far side of the room. She could smell the whisky on his breath. He cursed as she desperately raked one side of his face with her fingernails.

Jackson ran up behind Wilson, plucked the Circle B hand's gun from its holster, and threw it into the far corner of the room. Then he quickly hooked his fingers into the back of Wilson's gunbelt, pulled him backwards through the doorway with all his strength, and flung him to the ground. Wilson reached for his gun, then realized that it was missing. Slowly, he rose to his feet, glaring at Jackson. 'What a swine you are, Wilson,' said Jackson, 'attacking a defenceless woman in her own home. I aim to teach you a lesson.'

He drew his gun and handed it to Carmen who was standing, trembling, in the doorway. Then he faced Wilson again. The Circle B hand was well known to the other ranch hands as a formidable rough-and-tumble fighter who relied on brute force and flailing fists for his many conquests. He faced up to Jackson with confidence.

But in his first wild rush at his opponent he failed to make contact. Seemingly, Jackson melted away before him. The same thing happened again and this time Jackson delivered a heavy punch to the side of

Wilson's jaw as he blundered past.

Wilson was knocked sideways and fell to the ground. The hotel owner, Bellamy, who had seen the ruckus from one of the rear windows of the hotel, came round to observe more closely what was happening.

The fight did not last much longer. Wilson failed to land any solid blows on his elusive opponent, while Jackson landed a series of heavy punches to the face and ribs, and finally administered the coup de grace with a blow to the solar plexus. This left Wilson lying, doubled up, on the ground, and showing no inclination to continue the fight.

Jackson walked up to Carmen and took back his gun. Bellamy followed him.

'Are you all right, Carmen?' asked Jackson.

Still visibly shaken by the experience, she nodded. 'You came just in time, *señor*,' she said.

'This man will not trouble you again, Carmen,' said Jackson. 'I will see to that.'

After Bellamy had had a few words with

Carmen, Jackson held his gun on Wilson and ordered him to his feet. The Circle B hand rose with some difficulty and stood, bent in the middle, with his hands to his stomach.

'You come anywhere near this lady again, Wilson,' said Jackson, 'and I'll come after you. Let's go and see the marshal.'

He walked up to Wilson and prodded him in the back with the muzzle of his Peace-maker. Then, with the Circle B hand walking painfully in the lead, he and Bellamy followed him to the marshal's office. Several people out on the street watched the procession with interest.

Tomlin was sitting at his desk when they entered. He goggled at the sight of Wilson walking in at gunpoint, with Jackson and Bellamy behind him.

'I figure you'll want to jail this man, Marshal,' said Jackson. 'He forced his way into the home of Señora Alvaro and attacked her. It was lucky I happened to be nearby at the time and saw what was happening.'

Tomlin looked at Wilson, whose face was bleeding on both sides, and who was still bending over and holding his stomach with both hands.

'You did this to him?' he asked Jackson.

'I did,' replied Jackson, 'and I can tell you, I got a heap of pleasure out of doing it.'

'I can't go jailing people for no good reason,' blustered Tomlin. 'These cowhands don't get a lot of excitement out on the range, and they tend to cut loose a bit in town. But it's all innocent fun.'

'Innocent fun!' said Jackson. 'This man broke down the door of Señora Alvaro's shack and forced her down on to her bed. I don't see anything innocent about that.'

Bellamy cut in.

'Wilson's been pestering Señora Alvaro for a long time,' he said. 'Clem Brown says he told you about it. This man belongs in a cell while you decide what to do with him. If he goes free, folks here will be wondering if you've any regard for the safety of the womenfolk around here.'

Tomlin flushed with anger. He hesitated for a moment, then got up and escorted Wilson through a door and into one of the cells at the rear of the building. Then, scowling, he returned to Jackson and Bellamy.

'I reckon I'll have to get Doc Osborne to come and take a look at Wilson,' he said. 'You sure gave him the works, Hawke.'

'I was pretty well on the way to losing my temper,' said Jackson.

'You figuring on leaving Bedlam soon?' asked Tomlin. 'I'm getting tired of all the trouble you're causing around here.'

'I've got a few loose ends to tie up first,' said Jackson. 'When I've solved the mystery of what happened to my father, you'll be the first to know.'

As Jackson and Bellamy left his office, Tomlin looked after them. His brow was furrowed in thought. He was a worried man. Jackson and his companion returned to Carmen's shack.

'The marshal has put Wilson into a cell,'

Jackson told her, 'and you heard me tell him not to bother you again. I think you have nothing more to fear from him.'

'I thank you, *señor*,' she said, 'for all you have done for me.'

FIVE

The following morning, after breakfast, Jackson went for his horse and rode out of town for his appointment with Boone at the Circle B. He knew that there was a possibility that he might be riding into an ambush.

He thought back to his previous ride out to the ranch, and he could think of only one point on the trail where an ambush would stand a reasonable chance of success. This was about two miles east of town, where the trail skirted the south side of a large rock outcrop some thirty feet high and sixty feet in diameter. He thought that it would be possible to hide on or behind the outcrop, without being observed from the trail.

Just outside town he veered to the north, then circled round till he was approaching the outcrop from the north. From a concealed position, with the aid of his field-glasses, he studied the top of the outcrop and the side remote from the trail. He could see no sign of men or horses.

Satisfied, he returned to the trail and headed towards the ranch. He had travelled no more than a mile when he saw, ahead of him, two men close to the trail. They were Circle B ranch hands Riley and Mooney. They were kneeling by a cow which had been roped and hogtied, and was lying on its side on the ground.

As Jackson drew closer, he could see that the two men, both tough-looking char-acters, were unarmed. He stopped as he reached them, and the two men rose to their feet and stood side by side, facing him. It was a warm day and the two men's vests were lying on the ground close by. Mooney spoke to Jackson.

'Howdy, stranger' he said. 'You'll soon be passing close by the Circle B ranch house if you stay on this trail. We'd take it kindly if you'd call in and pass on a message to the ramrod, Hal Ford.'

'Howdy,' said Jackson. 'Be glad to. What's the message?'

'Tell him,' said Mooney, 'that we've got a sick cow here and we don't know what's causing it. We're going to look through the herd nearby to see if there's any more cows with the same problem. Likely we'll be late getting back.'

'I'll pass that message on,' said Jackson, and started moving along the trail again.

He had just passed the two men, who were both standing on his right, when he had a sudden presentiment of danger. He glanced back at the duo and saw that each of them had bent down and was picking up a revolver which had been hidden under a vest lying on the ground.

He had realized the danger just in time. He made a swift draw and shot Mooney in the chest before the Circle B hand was able to take proper aim. As the bullet struck Mooney, the ranch hand triggered his gun. The bullet passed close to the head of Jackson's horse, which suddenly reared, causing Riley's shot to go wide of the mark.

Before Riley could fire again, Jackson shot him in the chest. A moment later Mooney, who had collapsed on the ground, fired a final shot, seconds before he died. Jackson felt a sudden sharp pain as the bullet struck him in the side. He looked down at the two Circle B hands. Both were lying motionless on the ground.

Jackson dismounted, pulled his shirt out of the top of his pants and looked at the bullet wound in his side. The bullet, he was sure, was lodged in his body, and he badly needed to see a doctor. He stood still while an attack of dizziness abated, then he looked at Mooney and Riley. Both men were dead.

Painfully, he mounted his horse. He took

off his bandanna, folded it into a pad, and with one hand held the pad against the wound.

He knew that he must go into hiding as quickly as possible. It was clear now that Boone was in collusion with the marshal and his deputy. When Mooney and Riley failed to return to the ranch house with news of Jackson's death, Boone would send men out to investigate.

Jackson decided to head for a small grove of trees, well north of the trail, which he had noticed earlier when he was circling round to the outcrop. He would hide there until dark.

He headed for the grove, swaying a little in the saddle. He was feeling faint and the pain in his side was intense. He fancied that his horse was not running smoothly and he wondered if it had been struck by the bullet from Riley's revolver. He decided to check this once he had reached cover.

Half-way to his destination he blacked out momentarily and rolled sideways off the saddle. His mount stood near to him. The shock of the fall brought him round and he climbed slowly and painfully back into the saddle. When he finally reached the grove he rode to the centre, where there was a small clearing, and dismounted. Moments later, his horse collapsed on its side on the ground.

Slowly, Jackson knelt down beside it. He had been riding this horse for the past two years, and it had proved to be a strong and willing mount, never once letting him down. He could not see or hear any sign of life. Then he saw the bullet-hole near the shoulder, and wondered how the horse had survived long enough to get him there.

Saddened by the loss of his mount, he lay on the ground, holding the pad against the wound, and drifting in and out of unconsciousness. Soon after darkness had fallen, he decided to start out on the two-mile walk to Bedlam.

Groaning with pain, he slowly rose to his feet, took a look at the stars, and headed for town. The night was clear. He stumbled along at a slow pace, stopping to rest from time to time, and fighting a strong compulsion to lie down on the ground and abandon his attempt to reach Bedlam.

It took him two and a half long hours to reach the outskirts of town, where he stood resting for a while. To avoid the danger of being seen, he decided to head for the shack of Carmen Alvaro, which was set well back from the street. He would ask her to let Brown know he was there.

He walked slowly along the backs of the buildings lining the main street until he came to the Mexican woman's shack.

He saw that there was a light on inside. He stumbled up to the door and raised his hand to knock on it. But before his hand had made contact, his legs suddenly gave way, and he slumped to the ground. He tried to rise to his feet again, without success.

He dragged himself right up to the door and knocked on the bottom of it as hard as he could. It was opened a moment later by

Carmen. She shrank back when she saw the body lying on the ground. Then she realized that it was Jackson. She stepped outside, took his arm, and helped him to his feet. Then she half-supported him as he hobbled slowly into the shack and collapsed on the bed at the far side of the room.

Carmen closed the door, then pulled Jackson's shirt up. Her eyes widened as she saw the wound in his side. She spoke to him.

'I will go for Señor Brown,' she said. 'Soon, I will be back.'

She returned with Clem Brown ten minutes later. The liveryman looked at the gunshot wound, then spoke to Jackson. 'This ain't good,' he said. 'It needs a doctor. I'm going for Doc Osborne. You can tell us later on how you got into this fix. You don't need to be scared about Osborne letting Boone know you're here. He don't hold one little bit with the high-handed way Boone behaves around here.'

While waiting for the doctor, Carmen put some water on the stove to heat up, and cut off Jackson's shirt, using a large pair of scissors. She was just starting to bathe the wound when Brown and Osborne came in.

The doctor closely examined the wound.

'There's a bullet in there all right,' he said, 'and it's got to come out if Mr Hawke's going to stay alive.'

He opened his bag and took out the instruments he needed. Then he started to probe for the bullet. Jackson gritted his teeth and steeled himself to endure the almost unbearable pain caused by this procedure. His face beaded with perspiration, he gave a great gasp of relief as Osborne held in front of his eyes the forceps, with the bullet firmly gripped between its jaws.

When the doctor had finished treating the wound, and had applied a pad and a bandage, he spoke to Jackson.

'You're lucky,' he said. 'I don't think there's any internal damage that won't heal up naturally. So if there's no problem with infection, you should be reasonably fit again in two or three weeks.'

Jackson thanked the doctor, then gave a halting account of what had happened to him since he left town that morning.

'The marshal and his deputy, with some of Boone's men, have been searching for you,' said Brown, when Jackson had finished. 'They checked every building in town, just before dark. Tomlin's story was that you fired on two of Boone's men without warning, and killed them both.'

'They're bound to find my dead horse when they spot the buzzards,' said Jackson. 'Maybe they've done that already. Then they'll guess I can't be far away from that grove. When they can't find me outside town, likely they'll search the buildings in town again.'

'Until you're fit to ride,' said Brown, 'we've got to hide you somewhere where you won't be found.'

'I think I can provide a safe hiding-place in my house,' said Osborne, 'and at the same time I can make sure that the wound heals up properly.'

'Are you sure, Doc?' said Jackson. 'D'you want to risk making an enemy of Boone?'

'I want to do this,' Osborne replied. 'I've been wishing for a long time that I could help to put a spoke in Boone's wheel. If you can help me, Clem, we'd better get Mr Hawke to my place now. We'll take him along behind the buildings.'

'Before you leave, *señor*,' said Carmen to Jackson, 'there is something I must tell you. I have heard that you are looking for your father. On the night that he disappeared, I had finished my work at the hotel and I was walking to my house, when I saw three men and a horse behind the stagecoach office. They were lifting something on to the back of the horse. It looked like the body of a man.

'I stepped into the shadows and watched. One of the men got on to the horse and rode off with the body, and the other two went into the marshal's office.'

'Did you recognize the men?' asked Jackson.

'It was dark,' she said, 'but there was a moon. I am not sure, but I think that the man who rode off was Fisher, and the other two were the marshal and Boone.'

'The man who rode off,' asked Jackson, 'in which direction was he going?'

'To the east, *señor*,' she replied. 'I have not told of this before, because of the marshal. He is a bad man. I am afraid of him. I feared that if I said anything against him he would surely harm me.'

'Thank you for telling me of this, Carmen,' said Jackson. 'You can be sure that we will protect you from the marshal, if necessary. And thank you for helping me just now.'

The doctor and Brown helped Jackson off the bed, and, supporting him on both sides, they walked him to the doctor's house, making sure that they were unobserved. Inside, they led him to a room at the back of the house. It contained a single bed, a large chest, and a few small items of furniture.

They helped Jackson on to the bed, and

the doctor placed a blanket over him.

'Try and get some sleep,' he said, 'but before you do, let me explain how I aim to keep you hidden if the marshal decides to search my place again.'

After the doctor had explained his plan, he and Brown left the room, and Brown returned to the livery stable.

## SIX

The doctor looked in on Jackson a couple of times during the night and found him sleeping. When he went to see his patient in the morning, Jackson was awake. Osborne had a look at the wound.

'That's coming along fine,' he said. 'How're you feeling?'

'That wound's still paining me some,' Jackson replied. 'Otherwise, I ain't feeling too bad.'

'Rest is what you need,' said Osborne, 'but first, if you feel like it, I want you to take a little of this stew I just made. I guess it's quite a while since you ate anything.'

There was no sign of the marshal or his deputy in town during the morning, but shortly after noon Clem Brown called in to say that Tomlin and Fisher were searching the buildings further along the street, and were working their way towards the doctor's house.

Quickly, Brown and Osborne hurried to the doctor's bedroom. The big double bed on which he slept had drawers on one side reaching from underneath the mattress almost down to the floor. The drawers extended only half-way across the width of the bed.

The bottom end of the bed was covered by a sheet of timber, almost down to floor level, while the other side of the bed, and the top end, were positioned hard against the two walls meeting at one corner of the room.

The two men pulled the bed sideways

away from the wall, and placed a blanket on the floor near the wall. Then they helped Jackson into the room, lowered him on to the blanket, and covered him with another. Finally, they pushed the bed back in position, with Jackson effectively concealed underneath it.

Before Brown left, he and the doctor made up the bed on which Jackson had spent the night.

Half an hour later, Marshal Tomlin banged on the doctor's door. Osborne opened it.

'I'm looking for the man Hawke,' said Tomlin. 'Like I told you yesterday, he murdered two Circle B hands. I'm going to search your house.'

'Come on in,' said Osborne, and followed Tomlin as he searched each room. When they reached the doctor's bedroom, the marshal gave a cursory glance at the drawers in the bed, and the covered end. Then he closely examined the inside of the big wardrobe, before leaving the room.

He left the house shortly after, and Osborne, watching through a window, saw him meet up with Fisher on the boardwalk outside, after which Tomlin went into the saloon, while Fisher went into the blacksmith shop.

The doctor went to his bedroom, and pulled the bed away from the wall.

'It's all clear,' he said, then helped Jackson up, and supported him as he walked back to the bed he had previously occupied. Jackson collapsed on the bed, exhausted.

'Try and rest,' said Osborne. 'I don't reckon we'll be seeing any more of the marshal for a while.'

Clem Brown called in at the doctor's house during the afternoon, and he and Osborne went in to see Jackson. Brown told the others that Jackson's dead horse had been found, this being the reason for the town being searched again. After the second fruitless search, the marshal and his deputy had gone to meet up with some of Boone's hands for a combined search of the valley and, if necessary, the surrounding area.

'It seems,' said Brown to Jackson, 'that the marshal thinks that you were wounded when the two Circle B hands tried, according to him, to defend themselves. He found traces of blood on the ground well away from the two dead men, and reckons it was yours. Also, he found blood on the saddle of your horse.'

An hour after darkness had fallen, the marshal and his deputy parted company outside the Circle B ranch house with the ranch hands who had accompanied them on the search, and went in the house to see Boone.

'Any luck?' asked the rancher.

'Not a sign of Hawke,' Tomlin replied. 'We couldn't pick up his trail outside the grove. I'm beginning to wonder if he got hold of a mount somewhere, and rode out of the valley. All the same, we'll carry on the search for a couple more days.'

'I don't like it,' said Boone. 'You're certain he wasn't in town?'

'Certain,' replied Tomlin.

'I don't like the idea,' said Boone, 'that maybe he'll come back some day, and start causing trouble again. I can't figure out why Mooney and Riley didn't kill him like we planned. They were both pretty handy with a gun.'

'Maybe we'll be lucky,' said Tomlin. 'Maybe he's wounded so bad that he'll cash in his chips before he can get help.'

Over the next two weeks, at the doctor's house in Bedlam, Jackson continued to recover. Osborne was pleased with his progress, and thought that another few days would see him fit to ride again.

During his convalescence Jackson had thought up a plan which might help him to find his father. He was virtually certain now that Tom Hawke had been killed and was buried somewhere nearby, probably to the east of town. He had to find out where the body was located.

Clem Brown came in to see Jackson

occasionally, and he offered to do anything he could to help find the body of Tom Hawke. Jackson, grateful for the offer, because he needed the help of an accomplice, explained his plan to the liveryman and Osborne.

'I reckon I can manage to do what you want,' said Brown, when Jackson had finished. 'In fact, I'm going to enjoy it. I reckon it's a plan that stands a good chance of working.'

Three days later, the chance came to put the plan into operation. The marshal and his deputy, picking up their horses from the stable early in the morning, mentioned to the liveryman that they were riding out of town, and would be away for two nights. They didn't say where they were going. After they had left, Brown went to the doctor's house and passed on to Jackson and the doctor the information about the two lawmen's absence from town. At Jackson's request, Brown gave him a description of the lawmen's horses.

'They're doing just what we wanted,' said Jackson. 'I'll ride out of town tomorrow night. When I rode out to the Circle B, I noticed a piece of high ground to the north, standing inside the valley. I'll make for that, and I'll take my field-glasses with me.

'I figure that looking down from that high ground, I should be able to spot anybody riding in or out of town. I'll camp out there, and start keeping watch as soon as it's daylight.'

Jackson rode out of town at four in the morning, during the second night of the absence of the two lawmen. He was riding a horse loaned to him by Clem Brown. He was glad to be in the saddle again. On arrival at the high ground, he rested until daylight came, then kept a watch on the trails into Bedlam.

He had been watching for almost two hours when he spotted two mounted men approaching town from the north-east. Soon he was able to identify them as the marshal and his deputy. He followed them with the glasses as they rode into town.

When the two lawmen handed their horses in at the livery stable, Brown spoke to the marshal as he was about to leave.

'An old prospector called Murray rode into town yesterday,' he said. 'The way he was speaking, I reckon his mind was acting up. He came here to see if I had anything I could give him to slap on his burro to get rid of some lice that were driving it crazy.

'I gave him something for it, then he started talking about finding a body somewhere near here when he was prospecting. He said something about seeing a hand sticking out of the ground and signs that some animal had been scratching around it.'

Tomlin and Fisher exchanged glances. Both men looked concerned.

'Did he say just where that body is?' asked Tomlin.

'No, he didn't,' Brown replied. 'I asked him, but his mind seemed to wander off. I don't think he was right in the head. I told him that he should see you today about the body, and he said he would. But I heard later from the doctor that he'd seen Murray riding out of town in the afternoon, on the trail to the south.

'All the same, I reckon that if you want to talk with him it shouldn't be too hard to catch up.'

Tomlin grunted, and the two lawmen walked off together.

Brown could see that they were deep in conversation. Half-way to the marshal's office they halted, still talking. Then the deputy walked back to the stable alone, and took the reins of his horse.

'I'll be needing it for a while yet,' he said to Brown. Twenty minutes later, the liveryman saw Fisher riding out of town to the east. The doctor was passing by and Brown called him over and gestured towards the deputy.

'Looks like they've taken the bait,' he said.

From his vantage point on the high ground, Jackson also saw the deputy leave town. He followed Fisher's progress through his field-glasses, and saw him leave the trail leading to the Circle B ranch house, and strike off across the valley to the north. Then he disappeared into a pass leading through the ridge which bordered the valley.

Jackson scoured the valley below him with the glasses. He could see no riders. He went for his horse and walked it down to the valley floor. Then he rode east to a point half a mile west of the pass into which Fisher had disappeared. Turning north, he climbed the ridge.

Reaching the top, he rode his horse into a hollow, where he stopped and dismounted. Leaving the hollow he found a point from which he had a clear view of the rough ground to the north of the ridge. Carefully, he scanned the area with his glasses, but he could see no sign of Fisher.

He decided to stay where he was for a while. If he started to descend the north side of the ridge, and Fisher suddenly re-appeared, the deputy might well spot him. That was the last thing he wanted to happen.

Half an hour passed, with no sign of Fisher. Jackson was just about to abandon his position and move on, when a final sweep of the glasses picked up a rider who had suddenly appeared at the top of a distant rise, and was heading south towards the pass in the ridge. It was Fisher.

Jackson kept the rider under observation as he entered the pass, then emerged on the other side. It was soon clear that he was heading back to town, and it seemed to Jackson that the deputy's mission, whatever it had been, was now accomplished.

Jackson rode down the north side of the ridge and headed, with grim foreboding, for the point at which Fisher had recently appeared in view. When he reached the rise, he rode slowly to the top of the gentle incline, then paused and looked ahead.

The ground fell away in front of him, and about four hundred yards ahead, at one side of the trail, was a grove of trees. He rode up to it and dismounted. He estimated that the grove could have been Fisher's destination.

He would have had just sufficient time to reach it, stay inside a short while, then head back for Bedlam.

Jackson tied his horse to a tree, then started on a systematic search of the grove, covering it section by section, and looking for any sign of recent excavations. He was well inside the grove when he came upon a patch of ground which had obviously been disturbed over a small area. And here he spotted several human footprints.

He went to his horse for the shovel he had brought with him, and started digging on the patch. It was not long before he found the remains of his father, still clearly recognizable. Close by were the remains of his father's horse.

He stood for a moment, bringing under control the feeling of intense anger which was threatening to engulf him. Then, after checking that there were no banknotes in the pockets of his father's clothing, he located the two stab wounds in the back of the body.

Badly shocked, he stood motionless for a while, looking down at the body. Then he filled in the grave. He was sure that in a day or so there would be no indication that earth had been removed and replaced since the body was first buried.

Jackson stayed in the grove until after dark, sitting in sombre mood close to the grave. Then he rode back to Bedlam. Making sure he was unobserved, he rode up to the rear of the doctor's house and tied his horse to a post. Then he knocked on the rear door.

Osborne let him in, and Jackson asked the doctor if he would locate Clem Brown and ask him to come along to hear what Jackson had found. Fifteen minutes later, the doctor returned with the liveryman.

Jackson told them how he had shadowed Fisher and had found his father buried in the grove, with knife wounds in his back, and without the large sum of money he had been carrying with him. The two men expressed their sympathy.

'The problem is,' said Jackson, 'what to do

now? I'm one hundred per cent sure now that Boone, with the marshal and his deputy, were responsible for my father's death, and that their motive was robbery.

'But how do I prove it? Nobody actually saw my father being stabbed. Carmen saw three men in the dark, lifting something that looked like a body on to a horse. She thinks that the three men were Boone, Tomlin and Fisher. But was it my father's body that she saw? And was she right about the three men?

'And earlier today, when I saw Fisher riding back to town, I guessed he had been in the grove where my father is buried, but I didn't actually see him go in there.'

'I think you're right in what you suspect,' said the doctor. 'I've always thought it wrong that the marshal and his deputy should be in Boone's pay. But I never figured before that the three of them might be working together as criminals.'

'It seems to me,' said Jackson, 'that robbery and murder come easy to them. Is there much in the way of serious crime around here?'

'No,' replied Brown. 'The town's been pretty peaceful for a long time. There have been a couple of stagecoach robberies lately, but one of them was sixty-five miles south of here around three weeks ago, and the other was sixty miles north of here early yesterday. The stagecoach agent told me that both robberies were carried out by five masked men, and each time the shotgun rider was killed.

'According to the agent, both the stage-coaches that were held up were carrying shipments of gold dust a lot bigger than usual.'

'So there was a hold-up yesterday morning about a day's ride from here,' said Jackson, thoughtfully, 'and Tomlin and Fisher were out of Bedlam at the time. And they would have had time to ride to the scene of the robbery and back.' The doctor and liveryman both stared at Jackson.

'You're saying,' said Osborne, 'that the

marshal and his deputy could both be stagecoach robbers?'

'I figure it's very likely,' replied Jackson, 'and I reckon that the other three who joined up with Tomlin and Fisher for the robbery were Boone's men.'

He paused for a moment, his brow furrowed in thought, before continuing.

'Maybe we can prove what I just said about the marshal and his deputy. Does either of you happen to know if they were out of town when the first of those two robberies took place?'

'They sure were!' said Brown. 'I happen to know because the stagecoach agent came over to ask me where the marshal was. He wanted to ask him to keep a watch out for the robbers in case they called in at Bedlam. I told him that Tomlin had said to me that he and Fisher would be out of town for two or three days, and I didn't know where they'd gone.'

'Then the chances are,' said Jackson, 'that Tomlin and Fisher were involved in both robberies. If that's the case, how did they know that those two particular stagecoaches were carrying shipments of gold dust that were so much bigger than usual?'

'That's a hard one to answer' said Brown. 'I can't...'

Suddenly he stopped, then continued. 'I've just remembered,' he said, 'that about a year ago Tomlin's brother Jason came to see him for a few days, and the stagecoach agent told me that he worked in the big stagecoach office in Pueblo, as assistant manager.

'Maybe he had information about those special gold shipments that he passed on to his brother.'

'It all adds up,' said Jackson. 'What I'm going to do is ride to Pueblo. I'll set off after dark tomorrow, and on the way I'll call in at the Diamond H Ranch to see my mother. It ain't going to be easy telling her what's happened to my father.

'When I get to Pueblo I'll have a talk with the manager of the stagecoach office there. I'll tell him what I suspect. Then I'll try and persuade him to set a trap for Tomlin and the others so's the law can catch them red-handed.'

## SEVEN

Jackson rode up to the Diamond H ranch house late in the evening of the day after he had left Bedlam. His mother, about to retire, was startled by his arrival. As she rose from her chair in the living-room he could see that her face was lined with worry. She could tell, from her son's expression, that the news was bad.

They sat down, and Jackson told her of his discovery of Tom Hawke's body. She wept for a while, with Jackson's arms around her, before she spoke.

'I've been preparing myself for this news,' she said. 'I was sure something bad had happened to your father. Are we going to be able to catch whoever it was that murdered him?'

Jackson told her of his suspicions, and of his plan to catch the people responsible. Then he went to see Harley the foreman, and explained the situation to him. The ramrod was obviously badly shocked at the news of Tom Hawke's death.

'My mother and me,' said Jackson, 'we'd like you to take charge here, Pete, while I go after the people who killed my father.'

'Sure I will,' said Harley. 'Is there anything me and the men can do to help you?'

'If there is, I'll call on you,' said Jackson. 'Meanwhile, ask the men not to tell anybody outside the Diamond H that I've turned up here.'

'I'll do that,' said Harley.

Jackson went back to his mother and asked her if she knew of the location in Pueblo of the house where the stagecoach manager Harvey Grant lived with his wife.

'Yes, I do,' she said. 'Your father was a friend of Harvey's, and we've been in their house several times.' She described the house and its location.

'I'll ride into Pueblo now, while it's dark,' said Jackson. 'I want to see Grant without being spotted by anyone who knows me. I expect I'll be back during the night.'

It was well after midnight when Jackson reached Pueblo. He rode up to the Grant residence and tethered his horse round the side. He could see no light inside. He had to knock on the door several times before Grant opened it, in his night clothes.

Jackson explained who he was and said that it was important that he spoke with Grant. He apologized for calling at such a late hour.

'Come on in,' said Grant, a tall, pleasant-looking man with a neatly trimmed beard and moustache.

He led Jackson into the living-room, where they sat down. 'We heard about your father going missing,' said Grant. 'You have any news of him?'

'I have,' said Jackson grimly, and went on

to tell Grant of his father's murder. The shocked Grant expressed his sympathy.

Jackson said that he didn't want anybody in Pueblo, except the sheriff, to know that he was back at the Diamond H. Then he went on to voice his suspicions as to who had carried out the two stagecoach robberies. He had Grant's full attention.

'Did your assistant, Tomlin, know that each of those two stagecoaches was carrying an extra large shipment of gold dust?' asked Jackson.

'Yes, he did,' replied Grant.

'Then I reckon he got word to his brother in Bedlam,' said Jackson.

'I'm finding all this hard to believe,' said Grant, 'but I'm beginning to think you may be right. I've always thought there must have been a leak somewhere.'

'I'm aiming to try and persuade the sheriff here to set a trap for the robbers,' said Jackson. 'D'you reckon your company would cooperate?'

'I'm sure it would,' Grant replied. 'Losing

those two shotgun riders and two big shipments of gold dust was a big blow.'

'I know it's pretty late,' said Jackson, 'but d'you think you could get the sheriff to come over here now and talk about it?'

'I'm sure I can,' said Grant. 'Bill Sinclair's a good friend of mine. He lives next door. I'll probably have to wake him, but I'm sure he'll want to hear what you've just told me.'

Grant was back with the sheriff in fifteen minutes, and the three men sat in the living-room to discuss the situation. Sinclair was obviously excited at the prospect of bringing the robbers to justice.

When Jackson had fully explained the situation to him, the sheriff spoke.

'I've got to agree,' he said, 'that everything points to that rancher Boone and the two lawmen being responsible for the two stagecoach hold-ups, and what we've got to do now is catch them in the act.'

He paused to think for a moment, then continued.

'What we'll do,' he said, 'is feed the

information to Jason Tomlin through Harvey here that a certain southbound stage is taking on an extra large shipment of gold dust at Pueblo. And that's all the information he'll be given. The company'll arrange for the stage to arrive here without passengers, and I'll put deputies on board when it gets here.'

'I'd like to be one of the men working with you on this operation,' said Jackson.

'Glad to have you along,' said the sheriff.

'We've got to remember,' said Jackson, 'that one of the hold-ups took place sixty-five miles south of Bedlam, in New Mexico Territory. We've got to make sure, somehow, that this next hold-up takes place in Colorado, in your jurisdiction, Sheriff, and not in New Mexico Territory.'

'What I'll do,' said Grant, 'is tell Tomlin that the gold dust we're taking on at Pueblo is going to be offloaded at Belmont, a few miles this side of the New Mexico border, where it will be handed over to an escort of armed men. This should force them to hold up the stagecoach between here and Belmont.'

'I can rustle up the deputies without a lot of notice,' said the sheriff to Grant, 'but I guess your company'll need a while to get things organized. And we've got to allow time for Jason Tomlin to get word to his brother, and for Hank Tomlin and the others at Bedlam to get themselves organized for the robbery.'

'I expect to get the go-ahead from the company in Denver by the day after tomorrow,' said Grant. 'As soon as I do, I'll fix a date of nine days later for the imaginary shipment, and I'll discuss the shipment with Jason Tomlin. I reckon he'll pass the information on to his brother just as soon as he can.'

'Fine,' said Sinclair. 'Let me know as soon as you hear back from Denver.'

'I'll stay out of sight on the Diamond H until I'm wanted,' said Jackson. 'Nobody, apart from you two and the folks on the ranch must know that I'm here. If Boone and Hank Tomlin got to hear that I'm still alive, and back in this area, maybe they wouldn't be too keen on risking another robbery just now.'

'We'll both keep it dark,' said Sinclair, 'and we'll get in touch with you at the ranch the day before the trap's due to be set.'

The meeting broke up and Jackson returned to the ranch. Two days later, soon after the office opened, Grant received the go-ahead in a message from Denver. The message was coded, in case it was seen by his assistant. Grant casually mentioned to Tomlin that there would be an extra large shipment of gold dust from Pueblo to Belmont on the southbound stage in exactly nine days' time.

Looking out a little later from his small room at the back, into the big main office, he could see his assistant at his desk, busily writing something on a sheet of paper.

Tomlin was in charge of the process of collecting incoming mail, and handing outgoing mail to the driver shortly before a stagecoach left.

For the next half-hour, until nine o'clock, Grant worked in his room. Then he went out to Tomlin, and sent him out on an errand which, he knew, would occupy him for the next half-hour.

When his assistant had left the office, Grant picked up the bag lying against Tomlin's desk. He emptied the contents on to the desk, and searched through the pile. It was not long before he found what he was looking for.

The letter in his hand was addressed to 'Marshal Hank Tomlin, Bedlam, New Mexico Territory', and the handwriting on the envelope was unmistakably that of Jason Tomlin. Grant hesitated, then decided not to open the envelope, read the message, then re-seal it. If Tomlin looked at the envelope again before handing it to the driver, he might spot the fact that it had been tampered with. Grant was sure that he knew the message which the envelope contained.

Nine days later, Jackson, after receiving a

message from the sheriff, rode into Pueblo to join Sinclair and his deputies. There were eleven deputies present, including Jackson. Sinclair explained his plan for catching the robbers.

'I'm taking five deputies myself,' he said, 'and we'll shadow the coach at a distance to the west of it, aiming to keep out of sight of the robbers. When we see them closing in we'll do the same thing ourselves.

'The rest of you will travel on the coach with the driver. Five of you will ride inside, and one will ride on the box with a shotgun. That's what the robbers'll be expecting to see. I'm putting Jackson Hawke here in charge of the deputies on the coach. He's just finished a spell of service in the Texas Rangers, and he's the reason we've got a chance of catching these robbers. So take your orders from him.'

The stagecoach rolled in at nine o'clock in the morning, with no passengers. This puzzled Tomlin, because advice had previously been received from Denver that it would be full with through passengers. Five minutes before ten his eyes goggled when he saw the sheriff arrive with ten deputies, five of whom climbed inside the coach. Moreover, there had been no sign of a gold shipment arriving for loading on to the stage.

Tomlin slipped out of the rear of the stagecoach office and ran to the livery stable, where his horse was kept. Frantically, he started to saddle it, but was forced to stop when Jackson walked up behind him, and jammed the muzzle of his revolver into Tomlin's back.

'You ain't riding nowhere, Tomlin,' said Jackson. 'There's a cell waiting for you in the marshal's office. Let's go.' When Tomlin had been locked in the cell, Jackson ran back to the stagecoach and climbed on to the box beside the driver Ed Wheeler. Wheeler cracked his whip, and the coach rolled off.

Early on the morning of the day the coach

carrying the deputies left Pueblo, Hank Tomlin and Fisher joined up with three Circle B hands outside the ranch house, and after a few words from Boone the five men rode off to the north.

The place where the hold-up was to take place had already been selected. It was about forty miles south of Pueblo, at a point where a cluster of rocks on a small area of high ground west of the trail would provide them with cover while they were awaiting the arrival of the stagecoach.

They were within sight of this point when, as they were descending a steep slope, the horse ridden by Sadler, the Circle B hand who had helped Tomlin and Fisher to bury Tom Hawke's body, lost its footing and rolled over its rider.

One of Sadler's legs was severely crushed and he felt some pain around the ribs. Although it was clear that he could not take an active part in the robbery, Tomlin decided to continue without his help. Sadler's companions helped him into the saddle and Tomlin told him to ride into a nearby grove of trees and stay there until they picked him up after the robbery.

After parting from Sadler, Tomlin and the others rode on to the point where they intended to await the arrival of the coach. Just before they went into hiding there, they were spotted by a deputy who had been sent ahead by Sheriff Sinclair to look out for them. The deputy rode back to report their location to the sheriff.

Forty minutes passed before Tomlin and the others saw the coach approaching from the north, with a shotgun rider sitting on the box beside the driver. They waited until the coach had passed abreast of them, then rode out of their cover and headed for the coach, intending to come up behind it.

Jackson, who had been on the lookout for the robbers, spotted them and spoke to the driver, who reined in the team and brought the stagecoach to a standstill. The driver applied the brake, then he and Jackson left the box and climbed through the doors into the coach, to join the deputies already there.

The four robbers, as they came alongside, intending to fire through the windows of the coach, were totally unprepared for the hail of fire which came from the deputies inside. Nor were they prepared for the sudden appearance behind them, of Sheriff Sinclair and the remaining deputies.

In quick succession, the four robbers were brought down and lay on the ground, incapable of further opposition. Their weapons were removed and Sinclair put a guard on them. Then he checked up on his own men. The only casualties were a deputy called Latimer who had been in the coach, and Jackson. One of Latimer's ears had been mangled by a passing bullet, while Jackson had a bullet-graze along the side of his head, which had caused him to lose consciousness for a short while inside the coach, and had left him with a severe headache and dizziness.

Of the four robbers, two were dead, and the other two, Hank Tomlin and Fisher, both had gunshot wounds in the shoulder. Jackson identified the two dead men as Circle B hands he had seen during his stay in Bedlam.

Bandages were taken from a box on the coach and the wounds on the four injured men were bandaged. Then Tomlin and Fisher were bound, and hoisted on to the top of the coach while Jackson sat inside with the other deputies.

The coach turned, and headed towards Pueblo. Sinclair, and the deputies who had accompanied him, stayed behind for a while to bury the two dead men, then followed the coach.

When the coach reached Pueblo, the doctor attended to all the injured men. Jackson was advised to rest for a few days, and went to stay with his mother on the Diamond H. Tomlin and Fisher each had a bullet removed from the shoulder without any complications setting in. The trial took place nine days later.

When the case was heard, Jackson was

among the witnesses who gave evidence, and Hank Tomlin and Fisher were both sentenced to death by hanging. Neither of them made any statement involving Boone. Jason Tomlin received a long custodial sentence for his part in the affair.

After the trial and the hanging were over, Jackson went to see the sheriff in his office. Sinclair thanked him for his help in catching the robbers, and told him that on the return of the posse to Pueblo he had telegraphed the US marshal in Amarillo, telling him of Boone's almost certain involvement in at least two stagecoach robberies, and in the murder of Jackson's father. He had suggested that Boone be arrested and questioned.

Sinclair asked Jackson about his future plans.

'I've got to make sure,' said Jackson, 'that Boone gets what's coming to him because of what happened to my father. I'm setting out for Bedlam tomorrow to see what the situation is down there.'

# EIGHT

The injured Circle B hand Sadler, who had gone to hide in the grove just before the attempted robbery of the stagecoach, observed with dismay and apprehension the fate of Tomlin and the others, and prayed that the grove would not be searched.

As soon as the deputies had buried the two bodies and had ridden off to the north, he left the grove and rode south as fast as his injuries would allow. He knew that Boone must be made aware, as early as possible, of the foiled robbery attempt.

When he arrived at the Circle B, after a long, agonizing ride, and gave Boone the bad news, the rancher guessed that he must quit the ranch quickly if he wanted to avoid arrest.

He and his men, accompanied by Rachel,

all left the following morning, heading south-east for the Texas Panhandle. After crossing the border they headed east across the Panhandle. One of the hands, who had been sent by Boone to get some supplies at a small store in a town in the area through which they were passing, came back with the information that Jackson Hawke had been a member of the posse which had foiled the robbery. Boone cursed at the news that Jackson was still alive.

Sadler's injuries, which had received no attention from a doctor, were growing increasingly painful as the days passed, and he was unable to ride as quickly as Boone wished. By the time they were approaching the border with Indian Territory, he was suffering excruciating pain and frequent attacks of dizziness, and had fallen some way behind.

Boone told the others to carry on, then rode back to Sadler, who was hidden from view behind a small hill which the others had recently skirted. He found that Sadler had fallen from his horse and was lying unconscious on the ground.

He waited for a while, then pulled off Sadler's vest. Boone drew his revolver, wrapped the vest around it to muffle the sound, and shot the wounded man in the chest. Just before the hammer fell, Sadler's eyes opened and he stared up into the rancher's face.

Leaving Sadler on the ground, Boone rode back to the others. He told them that Sadler had fallen from his horse and wasn't able to ride any further. He said that with the law on their heels, they had no option but to leave him behind. There was a good chance that somebody would find him and get him to a doctor.

Soon after they had crossed the border into Indian Territory, the majority of Boone's hands decided to part company with him and go their own way.

When Jackson arrived in Bedlam, he made no attempt at concealment, and rode straight up to the livery stable around sunset. He found the liveryman inside. Brown was pleased to see him.

'We heard a while back about that trap you set,' he told Jackson, 'and we just got word about the hanging yesterday. You sure done a good job. Most of the townsfolk are glad to have seen the last of Tomlin and Fisher.'

'There's still some unfinished business to attend to,' said Jackson.

'I guess there is,' said Brown, 'if you're talking about Boone.'

'Is he still at the ranch?' asked Jackson.

'No,' replied the liveryman. 'We didn't know it at the time, but it turns out he and his men quit the ranch three days after you sprung the trap, and one day before three deputy US marshals came looking for him.

'I heard from a stagecoach driver yesterday that the deputies lost the trail of Boone and his men in the Panhandle, near the Canadian River, and about twenty miles from the border with Indian territory. The driver said the deputies had asked him to make sure that somebody in Bedlam told you about this, as soon as you got here.'

'Did his stepdaughter leave with him?' asked Jackson.

'Must have done,' Brown replied. 'We ain't seen her around since Boone left.'

'I've been worried about her,' said Jackson. 'The last time I talked with her, I could tell she was mighty troubled about something.'

'Funny you should say that,' said Brown. 'A week before Boone quit the ranch, his stepdaughter rode into town with a small suitcase twenty minutes before the east-bound stagecoach was due to leave. She left her horse here and bought a ticket. I noticed there was a big bruise on her face, and she seemed mighty upset. She looked like she'd been crying.

'She climbed on the stagecoach when it came in, but just before it left, Boone turned up in a buggy, with five hands riding alongside. He opened the stagecoach door and dragged his stepdaughter out and put her in the buggy. Then they all headed back towards the ranch.

'It was plain she didn't want to go with him, and maybe somebody would have tried to help her if Boone hadn't had five armed men with him.'

Disturbed by this news, Jackson decided to head for the point where the trail of Boone and his men had been lost. But first, he went with the town undertaker to his father's grave, where the body was recovered and put in a coffin which was to be shipped to Mary Hawke at the Diamond H Ranch in Colorado.

Two days later, Jackson rode up to the Canadian River in the Panhandle and started to follow the north bank of the river towards Indian Territory, enquiring as he went along, if there had been any sighting of a group of riders, one of them a woman, riding east a few days after Boone had quit the ranch. But all his enquiries proved fruitless.

A few miles from the border, still following

the river, he came across a lone homestead stretching back from the river bank. He rode up towards the house, then turned and headed towards the barn as he saw a man walk out of the building and halt, looking in his direction. Jackson stopped in front of the man.

'Howdy,' he said. 'My name's Hawke. I'd appreciate a few minutes of your time.'

He thought that the man looked at him rather strangely when he mentioned his name.

'You're welcome,' said the homesteader. 'Light down and come in the house. We don't get many callers here. My name's Randle, John Randle.'

Jackson followed him into the house, where Randle introduced him to his wife. He noticed that when his name was mentioned to her, Mrs Randle gave him the same strange look that he had received from her husband. He accepted her invitation to take supper with them later on.

Jackson told them briefly of his search for

Boone, and the events leading up to it. Then he asked them if they had seen any sign of Boone and his party. But once again he was disappointed. They had seen no sign of such a group of riders.

'But something else happened just around that time,' said Randle. 'Would you mind telling us your first name.'

'It's Jackson,' their guest replied.

'Jackson Hawke,' said Randle, reflectively 'I don't reckon there's likely to be many men with that name around.'

He walked over to a chest, pulled out a drawer, and from it took a sealed envelope. He brought it over and showed it to Jackson, who could see his own name *Jackson Hawke* scrawled on it in barely legible handwriting.

'This could be for you,' said Randle. 'Let me tell you the story behind it.'

He told Jackson that around the time Boone was supposed to have been in the area, he and his wife took a ride on the buckboard to visit friends living several miles upstream. They stayed there most of the day. On the way back home they came across a man lying on the trail, who told them his name was Sadler.

The man had been shot in the chest, and had an injured leg. He was barely conscious and seemed close to death. They had lifted him on to the buckboard and had taken him to the homestead. There was no doctor in the area, and they did what they could for the injured man.

In one of his lucid periods he had asked for a pencil and paper. Laboriously, he wrote on this for a while, frequently pausing to rest. Finally, he asked for an envelope, placed the sheet of paper in it, and sealed it. On the envelope he wrote the name 'Jackson Hawke'.

Exhausted, he had rested for a while, then he asked Randle to make sure that the envelope got to Jackson Hawke.

'I promised Sadler to do my best,' said Randle, 'and I asked him where this Jackson Hawke was likely to be. He said he weren't sure, but if I sent the envelope to a friend of Hawke's, he would pass it on.

'I asked him the name of the friend, and where he lived, and he was just starting to tell me this when his head flopped sideways and he died. We buried him on that little knoll behind the barn. I didn't know what to do with the envelope, which is why I'm glad you turned up here. I figure it was meant for you, and I sure am curious about the message inside.'

He handed the envelope over to Jackson, who opened it and took out the piece of paper inside. The writing on it was uneven and parts were difficult to read. Slowly, Jackson read out the message on the paper, for Randle and his wife to hear. It went as follows: *Because I had a busted leg I was holding Boone up, so he shot me. He thought he'd left me dead. I want you to find him, I want him to pay for what he's done. Fisher killed your father on Boone's orders. Body is in grove of trees by trail six miles east of Bedlam. Boone and some of his men heading for cave hideout in*

*Indian Territory about eight miles from Lasko. Hideout is used by Boone's cousin Jake Rattigan. Sadler.*

'It looks like the letter *was* meant for you,' said Randle. 'What're you going to do now?'

'I'm riding to Lasko after Boone,' Jackson replied. 'I ain't never been there, but I've heard of it. It's about seventy miles east of here, near the Canadian River. If I manage to find Boone and the others, I'll bring the law in on them if I get the chance.'

Jackson ate supper with the Randles and accepted the offer of shelter in the barn for the night. He rode off after taking breakfast and soon crossed the border into Indian Territory. Then he headed straight for Lasko.

He camped out overnight and rode into Lasko in the afternoon. He had decided to keep quiet for the time being about the reason for his presence in town, in case Boone or Rattigan came to hear of it. Handing his horse in at the livery stable, he told the liveryman that he was on the way to

Texas, but might rest up in Lasko for a few days.

He walked over to the hotel and booked a room, then had a meal in the restaurant next door. He kept a close watch for Boone and his men, in case any of them were in town. He did not wish to be seen and recognized at this stage. When he had finished the meal he went to his room in the hotel and rested on the bed for a while, considering the situation.

He decided that on the following morning he would ride eight miles out of town in an easterly direction, and would then start to circle the town slowly, at a distance of eight miles from it, looking closely for any sign of the hideout cave that Sadler had mentioned in his message.

Jackson stayed in his room until he went for breakfast in the restaurant the following morning. Looking out through the window on to the street as he was finishing his meal, he stiffened as he saw a familiar figure dismount outside the store across the street and walk inside.

It was Wilson, the Circle B hand he had thrashed when he was assaulting Carmen Alvaro in Bedlam. Maybe, thought Jackson, his search for the hideout was going to be easier than he had anticipated.

Quickly, he left the restaurant and went to his room in the hotel. From his window he could see the door of the store. He watched this until, five minutes later, he saw Wilson come out of the store, mount his horse, and ride off in an easterly direction.

Jackson went to the livery stable for his horse. He told the liveryman, Mort Jenkin, that it might be a day or two before he was back. He rode to the eastern edge of town, then dismounted. Pretending to tighten the cinch, he looked ahead, and could see Wilson cantering along the trail, to disappear behind a small hill in the distance.

He waited a short while, then remounted and followed Wilson, doing his best to keep out of sight of the Circle B hand. Wilson showed no signs of suspecting that he was being followed. When they had travelled about eight miles in a roughly easterly direction, Wilson left the trail and rode up to the mouth of a steep-walled gorge, where he stopped.

Watching from cover, Jackson saw a man suddenly appear at the top of one of the walls of the gorge and wave to Wilson, who waved back, then rode on into the gorge and disappeared from Jackson's view.

The man who had waved to Wilson also disappeared from sight, and it seemed likely to Jackson that he was a lookout, and that Boone and the others were holed up somewhere nearby. He could not follow Wilson into the gorge without being spotted by the lookout, and he decided to stay where he was until after dark. He settled down to wait, keeping the lookout's position under close observation through his field-glasses.

Darkness was starting to fall when he spotted a movement, and was just able to see the lookout climb down from his position and walk into the gorge. He waited for half an hour before riding halfway to the mouth of the gorge, where he tethered his horse well back from the trail, before proceeding on foot.

He climbed silently up to the position previously occupied by the lookout and confirmed that there was nobody there. Then he crawled along the wall at the top of the gorge, looking down into it for any sign of Boone and the others. He could hear the sound of running water below.

Dimly, through the darkness, he could see the opposite wall of the gorge, which appeared to be perpendicular down to the level of the water. After he had crawled about two hundred yards without seeing any signs of life below, he paused to rest. Then, just as he was about to move on, he saw what appeared to be the brief flare of a match coming from the opposite wall of the gorge, not far above the water level. It was not repeated.

Straining his eyes, he could see that the

flare had come from a circular dark patch on the wall of the gorge, and realized that there was probably a hole in the wall at that point. Maybe it was the entrance to the cave mentioned by Sadler in his message, and maybe there was a guard stationed at the cave entrance.

Jackson reckoned that it would be too dangerous to go down into the gorge to investigate the dark patch more closely. He decided to find a safe place, not too distant, from which he could, when daylight came, look down into the gorge with a clear view of both walls.

He went for his horse, and after searching for over an hour, he found a suitable place. It was in a cluster of rocks on the top of a stretch of high ground. He settled down there and waited for daybreak.

When it came, he looked down into the gorge. He could now clearly see the hole in the sheer wall, several feet above the water level. On the opposite side of the gorge there was a wide ledge between the top of the water channel and the wall of the gorge. There was no sign of Boone and the others. He settled down to wait and watch.

Ten minutes later, he saw the end of a timber structure slowly emerge from the hole in the wall, obviously being pushed from the inside. It gradually moved outwards until the end rested on the ledge topping the far side of the channel which was carrying water through the gorge. The structure was, in effect, forming a bridge over the fast-flowing water.

A man, not recognized by Jackson, emerged from the hole and walked over the bridge, then along the ledge running down the gorge. Jackson guessed that he was the lookout, heading for his station. He figured that if the lookout spotted unknown riders approaching during the daytime, he would run to give the alarm and the bridge would be drawn back into the cave, out of sight.

Jackson settled down to watch, hoping that some of the other occupants of the cave would soon show themselves. But it was over two hours before two men emerged and led their horses over the bridge, before mounting and riding out of the gorge. Jackson did not recognize either of them.

At noon, the lookout was relieved, but there was no other sighting of men or horses in the gorge until the lookout changed at 3.30.

Soon after this the two men who had ridden out earlier returned. Then, just as darkness was falling, the lookout returned to the cave and the bridge was pulled inside, out of sight.

Jackson decided to return to Lasko. The presence of Wilson indicated that Boone was probably present in the cave, but Jackson was not sure. Nor did he know whether Rachel was being held there. He decided to make a few discreet enquiries in town as to whether either of them had been seen in the area.

Arriving in Lasko, he rode up to the livery stable to hand his horse over to Jenkin, the liveryman. Jenkin was talking inside the stable to an elderly man, grizzled and frail. Their conversation ended when Jackson walked in and approached them. The old man turned and nodded to Jackson as he slowly hobbled past him and out on to the street.

'Poor old Daley,' said Jenkin, looking after him, and shaking his head. 'There's a man who started prospecting in California in '49, when he first got the fever. Ever since, up to six years ago, he roamed the West, looking for the bonanza that never came. What he *did* end up with was a bad attack of the rheumatics that he can't get rid of.

'Sometimes he can't move out of that old shack of his behind the saloon for days at a time. When that happens, I look in on him every now and again, to see that he's all right, and my wife cooks the odd meal for him.'

The following morning, Jackson breakfasted in the restaurant, keeping an eye open for Boone or any of his men who might recognize him if they happened to come into town. When he had finished the meal, he walked along the street towards the livery stable, to see the liveryman. He felt instinctively that Jenkin was a man who would be on the side of the law, and would give him any help that he could to ensure Boone's capture.

As he approached the stable, Daley, the old prospector, hobbled out of the door and started moving diagonally across the street, weaving slightly as he went. As Jackson was about to greet Jenkin he noticed that the liveryman was looking at a rider on the street who was just passing the stable at a slow trot, and was heading in Daley's direction.

The man was a stranger to Jenkin. He was stocky in build, and bearded, with a mean, scowling face. He looked as though he had been camping out on the trail for some time. His name was Carter, and he was an outlaw, wanted for a string of bank robberies in Kansas.

His last robbery in Ellsworth, Kansas, had

been unproductive. It had been interrupted by the arrival of a deputy town marshal. Carter, with a posse at his heels, and a flesh wound, where a bullet had grazed his buttock, had been lucky to escape into Indian Territory, where there was a chance that he could safely hide from the law.

Riding along the street of Lasko, after a long, painful day in the saddle, and with no gains from his latest venture, Carter was not in the best of moods. His scowl deepened as he looked at Daley, who had stopped on the street ahead of him, to rest his legs for a moment.

As Carter was coming up to pass Daley, the old prospector started walking again, but one of his legs suddenly gave way. He fell sideways, just in front of Carter's horse, which reared, almost unseating its rider, and greatly aggravating the pain in his buttock.

Cursing, the outlaw brought his horse under control, then turned it towards Daley, who had pulled himself to his feet and was standing facing Carter. Incensed, Carter pulled his gun and started firing at the ground close to Daley's feet. His third shot grazed the heel of his victim's boot and Daley yelled as he almost lost his balance.

Jackson ran up behind Carter, and before a fourth shot could be fired he yanked the outlaw out of the saddle and pistol-whipped him over the head as he was falling to the ground. Stunned, Carter lay motionless on the ground, as Jackson blindfolded him with his own bandanna, then used the outlaw's rope to tie him hand and foot.

He picked up Carter's revolver, and removed his rifle from the saddle holster on his horse. Then he looked at the group of onlookers who had gathered around. Jenkin was among them.

'Where can I put this man to cool off for a while?' he asked.

'We ain't got no proper jail here,' Jenkin replied, 'but there's an empty shack behind the stable where we can dump him. I'll show you.'

He helped Jackson to drag Carter round

to the shack, and they left him lying on the floor inside. He was just beginning to stir.

'I reckon,' said Jackson, as he and Jenkin walked away, 'that he'll be able to loosen off those ropes in an hour or two. I didn't tie them all that tight.'

Jenkin looked around for Daley, and saw him hobbling painfully off the street towards his shack.

'I'll see if Brad's all right,' he said, 'but first I've got a couple of things to attend to in the stable.'

'I'll go myself,' offered Jackson. 'I expect he's a bit shook up, getting shot at like that.'

'All right,' said Jenkin. 'I'll see you there later.' Jackson walked to the shack behind the saloon and knocked on the door. After a short while it was opened by Daley.

'Just called by to see if you're all right,' said Jackson. Daley beckoned him inside to a chair and sat down himself.

'Thanks to you, I am,' he said. 'I reckon that if you hadn't taken a hand, maybe I'd have stopped a bullet. I'm obliged to you.'

Suddenly, the thought occurred to Jackson that maybe Daley had done some prospecting in the area, before he settled down in Lasko, and if that was the case, maybe he knew something about what lay behind the hole in the wall of the gorge.

For a while he chatted with Daley about prospecting in general, then asked him if he had done any around Lasko. 'Sure,' replied Daley, 'it was about twenty years ago. I had a partner at the time, Ron Massey. He died eleven years ago. We spent a few months around here.'

'Yesterday,' said Jackson, 'in a gorge about eight miles east of here, I spotted a big hole in the sheer wall of the gorge, not far above the water level. I was wondering if you ever came across it.'

'We sure did,' Daley replied. 'I remember it like it was yesterday. As you can guess, we were sure itching to get inside and have a good look around.'

'Not an easy thing to do, I reckon,' said Jackson. 'Did you manage it?'

'We did,' Daley replied. 'Remember, I was a lot younger then, and Ron was about the same age as me. We left the gorge and worked our way round to the top of the wall above the hole. Then we made a rope-ladder and fixed it there so's it hung down across the hole.'

'What was it like inside there?' asked Jackson.

'As I recollect,' said Daley, 'there was a passage behind the hole which ran straight for a while, then curved before it ran into a big cave. There were passages from the big cave to three smaller ones. The roofs were all around nine or ten feet high.

'We both spent a long time in there, searching the place for any signs of gold or silver, but once again, our luck was out.'

'Sounds like it could be a good hideout for outlaws,' said Jackson.

'You're right there,' said Daley. 'I reckon there's room in there for two or three gangs.'

'I'll be leaving now,' said Jackson.

'Thanks again for what you did,' said

Daley, 'but before you go, if you're really interested in those caves, I can tell you that after all that trouble we went to, making that rope-ladder and climbing up and down it, on the day before we left we found another way in.'

'Another way in!' said Jackson. 'That is interesting. Where is it?'

'Above the hole in the wall,' said Daley, 'the ground at the top of the wall is level, but it starts to fall away as you move further away from the gorge. The entrance is on this slope.

'We found it from the inside, when we climbed to the top of the wall in one of the smaller caves to have a look at a recess there. At the back of the recess there was a narrow passage which couldn't be seen from the floor. I crawled through this passage into a bigger one which came out on the hillside.'

As Daley finished speaking, the liveryman came in and had a few words with him. Jackson knew that Daley must be curious about his interest in the caves, and he decided to tell him and Jenkin the real reason for his presence in Lasko. He was sure he could trust them both.

They listened in silence to his story.

'I've heard of the Rattigan gang,' said Jenkin, when Jackson had finished. 'In fact, they darned near killed a cousin of mine during a bank raid in Kansas. What's your next move going to be?'

'Now that I know there's another way into the caves,' Jackson replied, 'I'm going to go in there during the night and rescue the girl. Then, as soon as she's safe, I'm going after Boone.'

'This girl,' asked Jenkin, 'she's a friend of yours?'

'I'm hoping she's going to be more than that,' Jackson replied. 'I'm hoping she'll agree to marry me. But before I ride out there I've got to have a pretty good idea of where that other entrance into the caves is located. I'd be obliged if you could help me on that, Mr Daley.'

'Don't forget,' said Daley, 'that it's all of twenty years since I was in those caves. All the same, I reckon I can point you pretty much in the right direction. But even if you do get in, I guess you know as well as I do that getting the girl out ain't going to be easy.'

He proceeded to give Jackson as much information about the second entrance to the caves as he was able. Jackson thanked him, and left the shack with Jenkin.

'I'll ride out to the gorge after dark,' he said, 'and I'll search for that entrance. If I do manage to get Rachel out I'll bring her back to Lasko.'

'Bring her to us,' said Jenkin, 'for as long as you want. Beth is always craving for some female company.'

'Thanks for the invitation,' said Jackson, 'I'll do that. It would probably be a good idea to keep her hidden while Boone's still around.'

'We can arrange that,' said Jenkin.

'I'd like to get a message to my mother in

Colorado,' said Jackson. 'She'll be wondering how my search for Boone is going.'

'Write it down and give it to me,' said Jenkin. 'First chance I get, it'll be on its way to a telegraph office.'

'I'm obliged,' said Jackson.

An hour later, after handing the message to Jenkin, Jackson was talking with the liveryman inside the stable when they saw Carter, the outlaw who had been pistol-whipped earlier by Jackson, run past the side window into the street.

Holding one hand to his aching head, he ran to two townsmen standing outside the saloon. The two men in the stable watched from the door as Carter, cursing fluently, asked the two men if they knew who it was who had attacked him in the street. They both shook their heads. Then the outlaw ran over to the blacksmith, working in his shop, and received the same response.

Turning away, almost incoherent with rage, Carter ran over to his horse, to find that his rifle was missing from the saddle holster. He stood by his mount, looking up and down the street, undecided what to do next.

'Nobody's going to tell him,' said Jenkin, 'who it was that pistol-whipped him and took his weapons. I reckon he'll be moving on before long.'

## NINE

An hour after midnight, Jackson arrived at the slope on which he hoped to find the entrance to the caves. This slope was not visible in daylight from inside the gorge or from the lookout position.

It was dotted with numerous patches of brush, behind one of which was the entrance he sought. Using the information that Daley had given him he selected an area of search. There was just enough light to allow him to examine it, a strip at a time, stopping at each patch of brush to check whether or not it concealed an opening in the hillside.

He had almost covered the area he had selected when, forcing his way through a thick wall of brush, he found an opening on the far side. He paused for a moment, then walked through the opening into the passage beyond. Slowly he felt his way along the passage. After about twenty yards, his head struck the roof, and he was obliged to continue on hands and knees.

He stopped short as he saw a dim light in front of him, and listened for a few moments. Hearing no sound, he cautiously moved on again until he reached the recess in the wall of the cave which Daley had described to him. Cautiously, he inched forward and looked down into the cave.

By the light of an oil-lamp standing on the floor he could see three sleeping figures, blanket-covered, and spaced a few feet from one another. They were on the far side of the cave from him, and all three appeared to be sleeping soundly. He was sure, from their size, that Rachel was not one of them.

Looking closely at the floor of the recess in which he was kneeling, Jackson was relieved to see a feature on which the success of his plan depended. Projecting from it was a small pillar of rock around which, he thought, the end of a rope lowered into the cave could be tied.

He pushed hard against the pillar. It seemed firm enough for his purpose. Working in silence, he unwound a length of rope, knotted at intervals, from around his body, and tied one end around the pillar. The other end, he lowered down to the floor of the cave.

Seeing that all three men below still appeared to be sleeping soundly, he grasped the rope and lowered himself down it to the floor. Then he threw the rope back into the recess, leaving just enough hanging down for him to be able to reach it from the floor when he returned.

To his left, he could see a passage leading

out of the cave. He tiptoed over to it, and along it until he reached the large cave described by Daley. Peering into it, he could see two lighted oil-lamps and, on one side of the cave, three men lying asleep on the floor. Opposite them, on the other side, ten horses were tied to a picket-line suspended from two metal spikes hammered into crevices in the wall.

Jackson slipped into the cave, and moved several feet along the wall until he reached the nearer of the two other passages leading into the cave. He tiptoed along it and cautiously peered into the cave at the end of it. Almost immediately, he recognized the slim figure and long raven hair of Rachel, the sole occupant of the cave. She was lying on the floor, asleep.

Jackson walked in and knelt down beside her. He clasped his hand over her mouth. She started to struggle, but he held her firmly, and whispered in her ear.

'It's Jackson Hawke,' he said.

Looking into his face, she recognized him,

and stopped struggling. He removed his hand from her mouth.

'Come with me,' he whispered.

As she rose to her feet he could see that she was fully dressed. He took her hand and led her into the big cave, first checking that the occupants were still asleep. Then he led her to the cave he had entered first. The three men inside were still slumbering.

Treading carefully, Jackson and Rachel moved over to the wall of the cave underneath what Jackson hoped would prove to be their escape passage. He pulled down the end of the knotted rope and tied it around Rachel's body, under her arms. Then, exerting all his strength, he climbed up the rope, making as little noise as possible as his body brushed against the surface of the wall.

He pulled himself into the recess at the top, and turned to look down at Rachel. White-faced, she was looking up at him. He started pulling her up, while she silently fended herself away from the wall.

Finally, her shoulders rose above the bottom of the recess.

Simultaneously, they heard a snort from down below, and both of them froze. Looking down into the cave over Rachel's shoulder, Jackson saw one of the blanketed figures on the floor fling out an arm, then turn over from one side to the other, before continuing his slumber.

Jackson waited a few moments, then pulled Rachel up into the recess. Seconds later, carrying the rope with them, they were making their way through the passage and out on to the slope.

Jackson could see that Rachel was trembling, and for a while she sat on the slope, with Jackson by her side, and his arm around her. Then they went to Jackson's horse and rode off double in the direction of Lasko where, Jackson told her, friends were waiting for them.

On the ride to Lasko, Rachel told Jackson that she had become increasingly afraid of her stepfather, who had insisted on her coming to live with him, and refused to let her return to her own relatives back east. Also, he had begun to look at her in a way she didn't like, and had started making advances to her, even suggesting marriage at one stage. She had become very fearful of the future.

She also told Jackson that, although her mother had never said anything to her about it, she suspected that Boone had been ill-treating his wife for some time before her death.

Jackson told her that Boone had been involved in the murder of his father, Tom Hawke, as well as in stagecoach robberies, and that the marshal and deputy marshal of Bedlam, who had been helping Boone in his criminal activities, had been hanged after a recent robbery attempt.

'I knew nothing of all that,' she said. 'I couldn't understand why my stepfather was leaving the ranch. I told him I didn't want to go with him, but he forced me to.'

They rode into Lasko just as dawn was

breaking. At the house behind the livery stable, Jenkin answered Jackson's knock and ushered them in. Jackson introduced Rachel and explained how she had been held by Boone against her will.

'I sure am glad to see you both,' said Jenkin, then went to rouse his wife. Beth Jenkin, a plump, motherly woman, bustled in shortly after, and approached Rachel.

'You poor girl!' she said. 'It don't bear thinking about, you being held by those villains all this time. We've got a room ready for you. You can go in there and tidy up while I get breakfast ready.'

Later, at breakfast, Jackson told the Jenkins how he had managed to rescue Rachel, and she described her harrowing experiences since Boone had prevented her from taking the stage back East.

'What's your next move?' Jenkin asked Jackson.

'Boone's got to be captured,' Jackson replied. 'By now, he'll have found out that Rachel's missing, and my guess is that he and Rattigan decided that they had better leave the hideout pronto. They wouldn't want to risk being penned in there by the law.

'What I'm going to do is ride back there now, and see if they've left yet. If they have, I'm going to follow them. But I'll come back here first, to let you know.'

'What you're going to do is dangerous,' said Rachel. 'There are so many of them.'

'If they're there they're not going to see me,' said Jackson. 'I'm going to ride to a high spot where I can look down on the gorge through my field-glasses.'

Later, when he reached the high spot, he could see that the bridge was spanning the water in the gorge, but there was no sign of any of the outlaws.

He rode round to the slope from which he had entered the caves during the early hours. He pushed through the brush and moved along the passage. The cave into which it led was empty and he could hear no sounds.

After listening for a few minutes, during which the silence remained unbroken, Jackson climbed down his rope into the cave and cautiously explored the three others, as well as the passage leading to the hole in the wall of the gorge. It was clear that the previous occupants had all gone, leaving behind them the signs of a hasty departure.

Jackson arrived back at Lasko in the afternoon, and went to the livery stable. Jenkin invited him into the house. They joined Beth Jenkin and Rachel in the living-room, where Jackson told them that he had found the hideout empty.

'I'm going after them,' he said, 'before the trail gets cold. Stay here, Rachel, and I'll come back for you as soon as I can.'

'There's no need for that,' she said. 'I'm going with you.' Jackson stared at her.

'But Rachel,' he said, 'this could be a pretty dangerous job I'm taking on. I don't want you hurt. It's best that you stay here.'

'I'm going with you,' she said. 'I don't want to hang around here, wondering all the time what's happening to you. And maybe I can help you somehow. I'm going with you. It's settled.'

Helplessly, Jackson looked at Jenkin and his wife. 'Tell Rachel she should stay here,' he said.

They looked at Rachel's face.

'It'd be a waste of time,' said Jenkin. 'I reckon her mind's made up. But I've just had the notion that maybe I can get somebody to give you both a hand.

'A good tracker's going to be useful to you if you want to catch up with Boone and his friends. And I have a cousin who's one of the best. His name's Bender, Clay Bender. He was only a young boy when he was captured by a Pawnee raiding-party when he strayed away from the covered wagon that was taking him and his parents West.

'Clay lived with the Pawnees until he and other members of the tribe were recruited as scouts by General Samuel Curtis to help put down Cheyenne and Sioux uprisings on the Great Plains. There were Indian Scouts from other tribes as well, but it was generally figured that the Pawnees were about the best in the business.'

'A good tracker would sure help a lot,' said Jackson. 'Where's your cousin now?'

'In a cabin a mile out of town,' Jenkin replied. 'He's a man who likes his own company. He stayed with the army for ten years as a scout, then took a job as deputy marshal in Ellsworth, Kansas. He was badly wounded by a couple of bullets during a raid on the bank there, and his friend, another deputy, was killed.

'I persuaded him to come down here, where me and Beth could help him out while his wounds healed up. He'll always walk with a limp, but otherwise he's pretty near back to normal.'

'You reckon he's fit to ride with us, then?' asked Jackson.

'I reckon so,' Jenkin replied. 'He's been talking lately about leaving. And there's a good reason why he might jump at the chance of riding with you.

'You told me that Boone was with the Rattigan gang. It so happens that this was the gang responsible for shooting Clay down, and Clay actually saw Rattigan himself kill his friend. But the outlaws got away at the time. I'll take you both to see Clay now, to find out what he thinks of the idea of joining up with you.'

As they approached the cabin, located in a small ravine one mile west of Lasko, Clay Bender stepped out and awaited their arrival. He was a little under six feet tall, lean and muscular, dressed in pants and shirt. His hair was fair, his eyes blue.

Jenkin introduced Rachel and Jackson, and all four went inside. Bender could speak reasonable English, having to pause only occasionally to search for the right word.

Jackson told Bender about recent events, starting with his father's disappearance, and continuing up to the present time.

'I aim to catch up with Boone and hand him over to the law,' Jackson concluded. 'Like I said, Boone's with the Rattigan gang, and I know you have a score to settle with them. And we sure could do with a good tracker to help us out. We're wondering if you've a mind to come along with us?'

Bender, who had listened in silence, spoke.

'I'm glad you've come to me,' he said, 'because just this morning I figured the time had come for me to start a search for the men who shot me and killed my friend. What you've just told me will make things easier. When are you leaving?'

'We're leaving early tomorrow,' Jackson replied, 'in time to get to the hideout by daylight.'

'Good,' said Bender. 'I'll join you in Lasko before you leave.'

# TEN

Jackson and Rachel, accompanied by Clay Bender, arrived at the hideout just as dawn was breaking. Clay was in the lead, with the others following close behind. All three crossed the bridge and examined the caves, then came out and made their way down to the mouth of the gorge.

Here they stopped while Clay dismounted and closely examined the tracks left by horses in a patch of soft sand stretching in front of them. When he had finished, he walked up to Jackson and Rachel.

'These are the tracks of the horses which were ridden out yesterday,' he said. 'These are the ones we will follow.'

Outside the gorge the tracks swung south, and Clay left his companions and ranged over the grassy area ahead, keeping generally to a southerly direction. Jackson and Rachel followed him.

'I don't know how he does it,' said Jackson, who had been keeping a continuous watch on the ground. 'I don't see no tracks myself.'

Some time later, looking ahead, they saw Clay wave to them and point to a gap in a ridge just over a mile ahead. He headed straight for this gap, and they followed him. When they reached it, Clay was waiting there for them. Just ahead was a stretch of soft, bare ground, and Clay walked forward to examine this closely.

'They'd be aiming to find a blacksmith before they got much further,' he said. 'One horse has lost a shoe, and on another one a shoe has cracked.'

Neither Jackson nor Clay was familiar with the area, so they did not know of any places nearby where a farrier might be found. The tracks continued south, and with Clay ranging ahead, Rachel and Jackson continued to follow him. Late in the afternoon they saw him climb to the top of a ridge and dismount. Shortly after, he waved to them to ride up to him.

When they joined him he was looking towards the south. Following his example, they could see in the distance, on a flat stretch of ground, a small cluster of buildings.

'They camped here for the night,' said Clay, pointing to the remains of a fire in the middle of a group of rocks. 'And two horses, one with a rider, took off towards that settlement down there. One horse had a missing shoe, the other a cracked one.

'When they came back, both shoes had been fixed. In the morning, they took off to the south-east. I reckon they were going to circle round that settlement down there. They wouldn't want to be seen.'

'We might as well stay in the settlement ourselves tonight,' said Jackson. 'It's going to be dark soon. We'll make an early start tomorrow.'

They rode down to the settlement,

gleaning from a weather-beaten signpost on the trail that its name was Broken Lance. Arriving there, they rode up to the blacksmith shop. The blacksmith confirmed that on the previous day a man brought two horses in for new shoes to be fitted. Before riding off he had bought a sackful of supplies at the store. He described the stranger as a big man, tough-looking and red-haired, who had given no hint of his destination or where he was from.

'Sounds like Wilson,' said Jackson, as they walked away from the blacksmith.

During the evening, at Rachel's request, Jackson showed her how to handle the Colt .45 revolver and the Winchester .44 rifle that she had insisted on bringing with her when they left Lasko. He soon discovered that she was an apt pupil.

They left Broken Lance early in the morning, heading south-west, and a couple of miles out of town they paused for a while to give Rachel some target practice. Jackson was impressed by her performance, after such a short acquaintance with the weapons.

Three miles further on, Clay picked up the trail of their quarry now heading south again. They followed it all day, and also the following day, until an hour before dark, when they breasted a rise and saw in the distance a flat-topped hill, with gently sloping sides.

Clay beckoned to them to turn and ride back a little way down the slope, where they dismounted.

'I see smoke,' he said, 'on top of that hill. Not Indian smoke.'

He and Jackson crawled back to the top of the rise and lay there, looking at the top of the distant hill. Jackson strained his eyes, but for a while could see no sign of smoke. Then, the slightest of wisps caught his eye, only to disappear almost immediately.

'The smoke is from a camp-fire,' said Clay. 'Perhaps we have caught up with the men we're after. Later, when it is dark, I will go and see. Maybe I will not be back till daylight.'

'Right,' said Jackson. 'We'll wait here for you.'

He proceeded to give Clay an accurate description of Boone, then the three of them rode back down the rise and made camp in a small rock-strewn hollow at its foot. Clay left two hours later, and Rachel and Jackson sat together by a small camp-fire. At her request, he repeated his earlier demonstration of the use of her revolver and rifle.

When this was over, they sat talking.

'What will you do,' she asked him, 'when you have caught up with my stepfather and handed him over to the law?'

'I'm not sure,' Jackson replied. 'First of all, I'll have to go back to the Diamond H and see if my mother wants to carry on at the ranch. If she does, likely she'll need my help for a while. I *had* figured on getting a lawman's job in Colorado, but maybe that'll have to wait.

'How about you? I guess you're figuring on hightailing it back East just as soon as you can.'

'That's how I felt a while back,' she replied, 'but I'm not so sure now. Despite what's happened to me here, I'm beginning to like the West. And back East I was getting a bit bored with...'

She paused as Jackson suddenly held his finger to his lips and sat in silence for a short while, turning his head from side to side and listening intently. He got up and walked around the campsite, his Peacemaker in his hand. Then he returned to Rachel, sheathing his revolver.

'Thought I heard something,' he said, 'and I had the feeling that there was somebody around, but I can't see anything to worry about.'

He sat down again, and she continued the conversation.

'As I was saying.' she said, 'I was getting bored with life in the East before I came back here, and I reckon I'd like to stay out here if I can. The problem is, I've got no home here now. Where would I go?'

'That's no problem,' Jackson replied.

'When this is all over, I'd like to take you to meet my mother, if that's all right with you.'

'I'd like that,' she said, 'so long as your mother doesn't feel that I share some of the blame for your father's death.'

'My mother's not like that,' said Jackson. 'She'll figure like I do, that nobody could blame you for what your stepfather did.'

Shortly after this they both turned in, lying not far from the fire. Jackson, still bothered by the same sense of unease which he had felt earlier, lay awake for a while, wondering how Clay was faring. Then he dozed for a spell, until an alien sound brought him instantly awake.

Rising on his elbow, he saw two Comanche braves, one on each side of him, rushing in his direction from the shelter of some rocks. A third brave was running towards Rachel.

Jackson grabbed for his revolver on the ground beside him, but before he could cock and level it the two Indians were upon him. One engaged him on one side, attacking him with his tomahawk, while the other struck him a blow behind the ear with his war club. Stunned, Jackson fell back on the ground, where his hands were quickly tied together.

Rachel did not wake until the Indian grabbed her. She struggled, to no avail, while her hands were being tied. Distraught, she looked over at Jackson, lying motionless on the ground. Then two more Indians rode up. Jackson was slung over the back of his horse, with hands and feet tied, and Rachel was ordered on to her own mount.

Taking the weapons of their captives, together with their food supplies, the Comanches, with two of them leading the horses of Jackson and Rachel, followed their leader Red Horse as he rode westward.

When Jackson came to, dawn was breaking, and he found himself looking down at the ground to one side of his horse. His head was throbbing with pain. Looking ahead, he caught a glimpse of Rachel, astride her mount, and breathed a sigh of relief.

He was surprised that he himself had not already been killed and left at the spot where they were attacked, and he wondered where they were being taken. Two hours later they came to a halt and Jackson was pulled off his horse and dropped on the ground.

He sat up and looked around him. He could see that they were in a small ravine. Rachel dismounted and ran over to him.

'Are you all right?' she asked.

'Apart from a bump on the head and a bad headache, I'm fine,' he replied.

Red Horse came over and spoke to Jackson.

'We have brought you here, white man,' he said, 'so that when our friends join us here two days from now, we can all watch you die. You will hang above a fire, and death will come very slowly. As for the woman, I will take her for my wife.'

Before he could continue, Black Feather, one of his companions, stepped forward and spoke. He was a powerfully built brave, with a sullen expression. He had long resented the fact that all the members of the marauding band of Comanches, except himself, tacitly accepted Red Horse as their leader.

'Red Horse has two wives already,' he said, angrily. 'Black Feather had one, but she has died. Black Feather will take the white woman.'

Red Horse's anger was evident as he drew his knife.

'The woman is mine,' he said. 'If you want her, you must fight.'

'I will fight,' said Black Feather. He drew his knife, and the two braves faced one another, each with a knife in his right hand, as their companions drew back to give them room.

For a while they circled and feinted without either of them drawing blood. Red Horse was lighter, and more agile than his opponent. But suddenly, as he stepped back, he stumbled over a loose stone lying on the ground, and Black Feather moved in to slash his opponent's right arm and retreat before Red Horse could retaliate.

Encouraged by this, Black Feather lunged forward again, aiming his knife-point at Red Horse's chest. But his opponent grasped Black Feather's right wrist with his left hand, twisted it, and pulled his opponent towards him, at the same time plunging the blade of his knife deep into Black Feather's chest.

Red Horse looked down at his victim, who was lying motionless on the ground, blood flowing from the wound in his chest.

'I will take the white woman for my wife,' he said.

Rachel and Jackson were taken over to a large boulder standing on the floor of the ravine. Rachel's feet were tied, and they were both placed in a sitting position, with their backs to the boulder.

The body of Black Feather was dragged out of sight further up the ravine, then the four remaining braves lit a small fire away from the prisoners and squatted on the ground while they ate some of the food they had collected before riding off with Jackson and Rachel.

Jackson spoke to Rachel, sitting by his side. He could see the fear on her face.

'Don't forget, Rachel,' he said, 'that we have a friend out there who's probably following our trail right now.'

When she replied, her voice was shaking.

'When d'you think he'll be turning up?' she asked.

'Some time after dark, I reckon,' Jackson answered, 'when he can sneak up without being spotted. It's a good thing Red Horse's friends ain't due here till tomorrow.'

During the afternoon, the prisoners were given a little food and water, but otherwise they were ignored.

After dark the four Indians had a meal, then remained squatting around the campfire talking to one another. Later, three of them lay down near the fire to sleep, with their rifles close by, while the fourth walked over to check the ropes binding the prisoners' hands and feet.

Then, after replenishing the wood on the

fire, he picked up his rifle and squatted down facing them, fifteen feet away, with his back to a boulder. He was obviously on lookout. Time dragged by as Jackson and Rachel watched anxiously for any sign of Clay. Then, at a few minutes past midnight, and with no warning sounds beforehand, Clay suddenly materialized at the lookout's side, clamped an arm around his neck, and drove a knife deep into his chest.

Clay recovered the knife and propped the dead Indian up, with his back against the boulder. Then he disappeared from Jackson's view, but seconds later, reappeared at his side and cut the ropes around Jackson's hands and feet. Then he did the same for Rachel.

Out of the corner of his eye, he could see that one of the Indians lying near the fire was stirring.

'Stay as you are,' he said urgently to Jackson and Rachel, 'and keep your hands and feet together.'

He pushed a Colt .45 revolver under Jackson's leg and laid the lookout's rifle on the ground against Rachel's skirt. Then he noiselessly retreated behind the boulder.

Red Horse, the Indian who had stirred, opened his eyes and sat up. Looking towards the prisoners, he could see that they were still in place. Also, the lookout was in position. Just about to lie down and resume his slumber, the Indian stared as the lookout slowly fell sideways onto the ground at the foot of the boulder and lay there motionless, with no sign of life.

Red Horse yelled to waken his companions, then reached for his rifle and rose to his feet. Jackson stood up with a revolver in his hand and Clay ran out from behind the boulder holding his six-shooter. Red Horse's two companions rose to their feet, grabbing their rifles.

The fight was short-lived. Jackson shot first, and his bullet struck Red Horse in the chest just as the Indian pulled the trigger of his rifle. The bullet from the rifle caused a slight injury to Clay's left leg. Before either one of the two remaining Indians was able to take aim with his rifle, Clay shot down one of them and Jackson dispatched the other. Seconds later, all three braves lay motionless.

Jackson walked over, picked up the rifles which the Indians had used, and took their knives. He dropped the weapons on the ground, well away from the bodies. Then he spoke to Rachel.

'You all right, Rachel?' he asked.

White-faced and trembling, and still holding the rifle that Clay had placed by her side, she nodded. Jackson walked over to Clay to look at the flesh wound on his leg. Bending down to look at it he could see that the wound was not serious. As he straightened up, Rachel noticed that Red Horse was moving.

The Indian pulled Black Feather's rifle from underneath a blanket lying on the ground close to him, and with a supreme effort, he started raising the barrel, with the intention of pointing it directly at the middle of Jackson's back. He had almost achieved this when the bullet from Rachel's rifle smashed into his head. Jackson whirled round, drawing his gun, to see Red Horse roll over, the rifle falling from his hands. He walked over to the dead Indian and picked up the rifle.

He went over to Rachel. Her face was ashen, and she was trembling. He took her in his arms until she recovered her composure a little.

'He was going to kill you,' she said.

'I know,' said Jackson. 'I had no idea there was a rifle anywhere near him. Lucky for me that you kept your head and shot him just in time.'

He turned to Clay.

'We figured you'd be along,' he said. 'Those braves jumped us in the middle of the night. I never expected to run into a Comanche raiding-party in this part of the Territory.'

'It was a surprise to me too,' said Clay. 'Glad I turned up here in time.'

He went on to tell Jackson and Rachel that

he had discovered that Boone and Rattigan and their men were camped in a hollow on top of the hill from which they had seen smoke rising two days ago.

'There were nine men in the hollow altogether,' he said, 'and I got a good look at Rattigan and Boone. I'm sure it was them. Maybe they're figuring on staying there for a while. If that's the case, we can get in touch with Fort Smith and get them to send a posse of deputy US marshals down here to arrest them.'

'You're right,' said Jackson, 'but the first thing we need to do is leave this place. Red Horse said he was expecting some of his friends here soon. We need to be a long way from here when they turn up. I reckon we should ride back to the area where you saw Boone and Rattigan.'

They arrived there in daylight, camping well away from the hill on which Clay had seen the outlaws. After dark, Clay rode off to see if they were still there. The news, when he returned, was disappointing.

'They're all gone,' he said. 'I'll pick up their trail again in the morning.'

They left camp at daylight and rode to the top of the hill. The other two waited while Clay looked for the horse-tracks of the departing riders. Then he waved them over.

'They rode off yesterday, down the south side of the hill,' he said. 'Let's go.'

## ELEVEN

Boone and Rattigan, blissfully unaware that Jackson and the others were so close behind them, had taken the decision to leave the hollow because the lookout had spotted what looked like a posse of fifteen lawmen riding in a south-easterly direction across the level ground below them.

Looking down at the group of riders, the two outlaw leaders were convinced that they were deputy US marshals, possibly searching for themselves.

'I don't like it,' said Rattigan, a short, slim man, with a sour expression. 'I reckon we should leave here after dark. And we should ride out of Indian Territory, and stay out until things quieten down. We could cross the Red River. It's only thirty miles away. Then we could hide out in Texas for a spell.'

'A good idea,' said Boone. 'Let's do that.'

They set off after dark, and when they reached the river they waited until dawn before crossing into Texas. They camped at an isolated spot on the south bank for two nights, then rode west along the bank of the river, intent on finding a more suitable hideout where they could stay until they judged it safe to return to Indian Territory.

They had ridden several miles when they came upon an isolated farm on the south bank of the river. There were no other buildings to be seen, in any direction.

As they drew close to the farm, they noticed a disused track leading down to the river. It led to an old crossing point,

Rafferty's Crossing, named after a rancher who had first driven cattle over it many years before.

Boone and Rattigan halted when they came abreast of the house, a two-storey, timber-built structure. They looked the place over. Apart from the house, there was a large barn, a corral, and two sheds. A small horse-herd was grazing in a nearby pasture.

'I reckon,' said Rattigan, 'that we could rest up here for a while. I'm sure we can persuade the farmer's wife to cook us some decent meals.'

'You're right,' said Boone. 'Let's go and introduce ourselves.'

He and Rattigan left the trail they were following and rode towards the house. Their seven companions followed them. As they came close to the door of the house, it opened and a woman appeared on the doorstep.

She was Ellen Webster, who was running the farm with her husband, Jim. They had moved west from Tennessee four years previously, and had settled happily here. They were farming 200 acres of land, and were raising quarter horses, much in demand by Texas cattle-ranchers.

Ellen, a handsome woman in her mid-thirties, looked, with some apprehension, at the nine riders in front of her. All were strangers, and there was a rough and menacing look about them.

'Is there a man around?' asked Rattigan curtly.

'My husband went to town for supplies,' she replied. 'He should be back soon.'

'What's his name?' asked Rattigan.

'Webster,' she replied, 'Jim Webster. What d'you want with him?'

Ignoring her, Rattigan told the men behind him and Boone to put all nine horses in the barn, and to stay in there with them, except for one man who would keep watch for the return of the farmer.

The woman suddenly turned and ran inside. Boone jumped off his horse and followed her, just in time to wrest from her hands a rifle which she had lifted off the wall. He struck the side of her face with the rifle butt, knocking her to the floor.

As she lifted herself to a sitting position, with her back against the wall, Rattigan came in and checked that there was nobody in any of the other rooms in the house. Then he came and stood by Boone, looking down at the woman. There was a trickle of blood down her cheek.

'You'd better get used to our company,' said Rattigan. 'We aim to stay with you for a spell and enjoy some home cooking. It's a while since any of us had a good meal. You do some fancy cooking for us, and we'll be a lot better-tempered. And a good time to start would be right now, unless you want another knock on the face.'

Ellen Webster slowly rose to her feet and stood facing them, swaying slightly. When her head cleared, she moved to a small table near the stove and started to prepare a meal. Her mind was filled with foreboding as to what might happen when her husband returned.

The meal had been prepared and eaten by the time the lookout spotted a buckboard approaching from the west, with a man and a child on the driving-seat. The buckboard turned off the trail and headed for the house. Inside the house, Boone held a gun against Ellen Webster's face.

'Don't even think of yelling,' he said.

Jim Webster, a clean-shaven, well-built man in his early forties, stopped the buckboard outside the house, surprised that his wife had not run out to greet them. He climbed down from the buckboard, reached up for his six-year-old daughter Sally, and lowered her to the ground. She ran to the door of the house, opened it, and went inside.

Following his daughter in, Webster came to a sudden halt as he saw three strangers inside. One of them, Boone, was holding a gun to his wife's head, and another one, Wilson, was restraining his daughter. The third man, Rattigan, spoke to him.

'Us three,' he said, 'and another six men in the barn, aim to stay with you for a while, Webster. The only thing is, we don't want anybody else but you three to know that we're here.

'If anybody *does* find out, especially the law, we ain't got no option but to take it out on the girl and the woman here. You can see we've had to give the woman a lesson already.'

Seething with anger, Webster looked at his wife's bleeding face.

'Who *are* you?' he asked.

'None of your business,' Rattigan replied. 'You get many visitors here?'

'Not many,' replied Webster. 'Now and again a neighbour calls, and a man rides out from Big Rock once a week to help me out on the farm. He stays for three days. He's due the day after tomorrow.'

'If we see anybody heading this way, we'll take the girl into the barn with us,' said Rattigan, 'so you'd better get rid of them pronto if you want her to stay healthy. And tomorrow you'd better drive the buckboard into town and get a lot more supplies. You're going to need them. And while you're there, you can tell the hired hand he ain't needed out here for a while. Think up a good excuse.

'The woman and child'll stay here with us, and remember what I said about what'll happen to them if you tell anybody we're here.

'During the night the three of you'll sleep in one bedroom, and there'll be a guard downstairs who'll have orders to shoot if he sees any of you trying to escape.'

Later, when Webster and his wife were in the bedroom with Sally, and after the child had gone to sleep, they discussed the situation.

'We ain't got no option,' said Jim Webster, 'but to do exactly what these men want. I reckon they're all outlaws on the run. If we cross them, who knows what they might do to you and Sally.'

'All right, Jim,' his wife said, 'but I'm

praying that their stay's going to be a short one.'

'Amen to that,' said her husband.

Clay, with Rachel and Jackson riding behind him, was able to follow the tracks of Boone and the others up to the north bank of the Red River. They forded the river, and Clay found the place on the south bank where the outlaws had camped for two nights, before riding on westward.

'I can't figure out where Boone and the others are heading,' said Jackson. 'I was sure they were going to hide out in Indian Territory.'

Some time later, following the tracks westward along the trail, they saw the Webster farm in the distance. When they came abreast of the farm, Clay looked down at the surface of the track leading off to the house.

'Don't stop!' Clay said to his companions. 'Rattigan and the others all turned off here and rode along that track leading to the farmhouse. And I'm pretty sure they're still there. Likely they've got somebody watching us. Let's ride on till we're out of sight of the farm. Then we'll find some place where we can watch it from cover.'

A mile further on, they rounded a flat-topped hill, and stopped on the far side. They dismounted, climbed the hill, and lay spread-eagled on the top. Jackson watched the farm through his field-glasses.

For a time they saw no action. Then a number of men walked from the barn to the house, to reappear forty minutes later and walk back to the barn. Soon after this, a man hitched a couple of horses to a buckboard, then drove it off the farm and along the trail towards them.

Clay and his companions descended the hill and waited at the bottom for the buckboard to appear in view. When it rounded the hill, they walked out on to the trail in front of it, and called on the driver to stop.

Webster pulled up hastily and stared at the

armed men and woman in front of him. From the driver's appearance, Jackson was sure that he must be the farmer. He walked up to the buckboard.

'You running the farm a mile east of here?' he asked.

Webster nodded. 'I'm Jim Webster,' he said. 'What d'you want?'

'We're chasing after a bunch of outlaws,' said Jackson, 'nine men altogether, and we happen to know they're on your place. We aim to hand them over to the law.'

Webster paled visibly 'You're mistaken,' he said. 'There ain't nobody on the farm but my wife and our six-year-old daughter.'

'My friend Clay here,' said Jackson, 'was an Army scout. He's followed the tracks of the horses those nine men were riding clear across Indian Territory to the Red River and on to your farm. There's no doubt in our minds that they're there.

'We're guessing that they've made threats against your family if you let anybody know that they're hiding on the farm. It's the sort of thing they *would* do. They're led by two men, Rattigan and Boone.

'But what my friends and I figure on doing is to get all three of you away from the farm into a safe place before we set the law on them.'

Webster looked at them, uncertainly.

'Can you do that?' he asked. 'My wife and me, we've been worried sick since they turned up yesterday.'

'We can do it,' said Jackson, 'but we need your help. Where are you going now?'

'Into Big Rock, about five miles west of here,' Webster replied. 'They told me to go and get some more food supplies.'

'How did they guard you last night?' asked Clay.

'My wife and daughter and myself slept upstairs in the big bedroom, with the door locked on the outside,' Webster replied. 'And judging from a conversation I heard between the two men who seemed to be the leaders, the bigger of these two slept in the small bedroom next door to us, and the other one slept in the living-room.

'Another man sat in the living-room on guard all night, starting at ten in the evening. I think he was relieved every four hours. The rest of the men slept in the barn.'

'Give us a rough idea of the layout of the inside of the house,' asked Jackson, 'and tell us a bit about the inside of the barn.'

After Webster had complied, Jackson thought for a moment before speaking again.

'You carry on to Big Rock,' he said, 'and get the things you want. We'll wait in those trees over there, and work out a plan to get you all away from those outlaws.'

He pointed to a grove of trees about 500 yards north of the trail and out of sight of the Webster farm. 'When you come back, drive the buckboard up to the grove. We'll be watching out for you. We'll have a talk about our plan, then you can carry on to the farm. But before you go, tell me, how is the barn door fastened from the outside?'

'There's a thick piece of timber that drops

into four metal supports and spans the two halves of the door,' Webster explained. 'When it's not being used, it lies outside on the ground, at the foot of the wall.'

'If the door's fastened on the outside, is there any other way of getting out of the barn?' asked Jackson.

'Only by battering the door or the wall down,' Webster replied, 'and that wouldn't be easy. I built that barn pretty strong.'

'Good,' said Jackson. 'Only two more questions now. First, d'you think you could get your hands on three or four sticks of dynamite while you're in town?'

'I reckon so,' said Webster. 'I got some there a few months ago to blow out a big tree-stump I was having trouble with.'

'Good,' said Jackson. 'You can hand it over to us when you get back. The second question is, could you get out of your bedroom through the bedroom window, if we helped you from the outside?'

'We could've done,' Webster replied, 'if only they hadn't nailed that window up real tight yesterday.'

'In that case,' said Jackson, 'let's talk about downstairs. Is there any way in there, except through the door from the outside, and the windows?'

'No,' replied Webster. 'There's no other...' He stopped abruptly, then continued: 'Come to think of it, there is,' he said. 'When we got here from Tennessee and built the house, there were still a few Comanche raiding-parties around. So I dug out a space under the floor that would take four people. The idea was that we would drop in there through a trapdoor if the Comanches set fire to the house with us inside. Then, if we were lucky, and the Indians didn't realize we were still alive, we'd climb up through another trapdoor outside the house when they were gone.'

Webster described the exact positions of the two trapdoors, and said he was sure that the outlaws had not spotted them. The one inside had a small rug lying over it, and the one outside was concealed by a small stack of timber lying across it. Webster said that if he got an opportunity of oiling the hinges on the inside trapdoor without being seen by the outlaws, he would do this.

Webster left for Big Rock, and it was almost sundown before he returned. He drove up to the grove. Jackson and Clay stepped out with Rachel, and Webster handed over the dynamite.

'We've got a plan worked out,' said Jackson, and proceeded to describe it in detail to Webster. When he had finished, the settler nodded approvingly, and he looked a little less worried.

'A good plan,' he said. 'I reckon it might just work. I sure hope so.'

'We aim to get into the house through the two trapdoors around half past midnight,' said Jackson, 'so you can expect to hear some action around then. We'll get to you as quick as we can.'

Webster drove off, and Jackson and the others settled down to wait until it was time for them to leave.

On the Webster farm, Matt Boone was not a happy man. On waking that morning he had experienced severe stomach pains which had persisted through the day. Soon after supper, when Webster and his wife and child had gone to their bedroom, he vomited and the stomach pains became more severe. He had a word with Rattigan alone.

'I'm getting worse,' he said. 'I'm going to see that doctor in Big Rock. Maybe he can give me something to help.'

'All right,' said Rattigan, 'but you'd better tell him you're just passing through.'

When Boone reached Big Rock after a painful ride, he stopped outside the hotel, tied his horse to the hitching rail, and went in to ask the owner, Trask, where the doctor's house was located.

'Straight across the street,' said Trask, 'over the store. There's some steps up to his place from the alley alongside the store. But he ain't in just now. Had to go and help a settler's wife deliver a baby. He's been away quite a while. Should be back before long.'

'I'll take a room, then,' said Boone, wincing as another severe pain gripped his stomach.

'Right,' said Trask, turning the register for Boone to sign, 'I'll give you one looking on to the street. If you sit near the window, you'll see his buggy out there when he gets back.'

Boone went up to his room and sat there awaiting the arrival of the doctor.


# TWELVE

Jackson, accompanied by Rachel and Clay, arrived at the Webster farm just after midnight, and they dismounted well away from the buildings. Then Clay noiselessly circled all the buildings to confirm that no outside guards had been posted. The only light he could see was behind curtains on the ground floor of the house.

He returned to the others, and they went to the barn door, found the piece of timber lying close by, and eased it gently in position to hold the door firmly closed. Then they walked over to the house, and carefully removed the timber which was lying on top of the trapdoor. The hinges were stiff, and care was needed to ease the door open without making too much noise.

When it was fully open, they lowered themselves down into the space beneath, and a moment later they were crouching under the trapdoor in the floor of the house. Jackson pushed one end slightly upwards, and they could see the light from an oil-lamp in the room above.

Looking through the gap, Jackson could see no sign of Rattigan or the guard. Webster had told him that they would not be visible from the trapdoor, which was in a corner of the kitchen area.

He pushed up gently on the door, and it moved without the slightest sign of a squeak. It was clear that Webster had managed to provide some lubrication for the hinges.

Jackson opened the door wide and climbed silently up into the room. The other two followed him. All three stood motionless for a moment, then Jackson moved forward until he could peer round the corner into the living-room.

The guard was sitting with his back to them, near the foot of the stairs. Rattigan lay motionless on a long couch, with a blanket over him.

The plan had been to catch the two men unawares and pistol-whip them both before going upstairs for Boone. But as Jackson moved forward, with Clay behind him, he trod on a loose board which gave out a creak loud enough to bring the guard to his feet, drawing his gun and shouting a warning to Rattigan.

Rattigan was not sound asleep, and hearing the guard's cry, he picked up the revolver lying on the couch by his side, and sat up to face the intruders.

Jackson shot Rattigan in the chest before

the outlaw could trigger his gun, and Clay gave the same treatment to the guard, who slumped to the floor as Rattigan fell back on the couch.

'Watch them, Clay,' said Jackson. 'I'm going for Boone.' He and Rachel ran upstairs and into the bedroom which Webster had said would be occupied by Boone. But it was empty. They went to the door of the adjoining bedroom, unlocked it, and went inside. By the light of an oil-lamp standing on a table they could see Webster and his wife and daughter on their feet on the far side of the room. All were fully dressed.

'We've taken care of Rattigan and the guard,' said Jackson, 'but Boone ain't in the bedroom next door. You got any idea where he is?'

'No,' replied Webster. 'He was in the living-room with Rattigan when we went to bed.'

'We've got the other men fastened in the barn,' said Jackson. 'Maybe Boone's with them. You'd better hitch up the buckboard and take your wife and daughter into town. They'll be safer there while we're dealing with the men in the barn.' They all went downstairs, where Clay told them that Rattigan and the guard were both dead. Jackson wrote something down on a piece of paper, which he handed to Webster.

'When you reach town,' he said, 'arrange for this message to be sent to the Ranger station at Fort Worth. It says that seven outlaws from the Rattigan and Boone gangs are being held here for them to pick up as soon as they can.'

'I'll do that,' said Webster, 'and I'll be back here to give you a hand as soon as I can make it.'

They all went outside and Webster hitched up the buckboard, then drove off towards town with his family.

Jackson went to his horse for the small sack containing the sticks of dynamite which Webster had brought him. From the ground near his horse he picked up two long slim poles which he had cut from a tree in the grove.

With Rachel and Clay by his side, he walked towards the barn, carrying the dynamite and poles. It was obvious that by now the occupants had become aware that they were fastened inside, as was evidenced by the sound of shouting and hammering on the door. A light was showing through the gap under the door.

Jackson took a stick of dynamite from the sack. He walked away from his companions, lit the fuse cord with a match, and threw the dynamite on to a patch of bare ground just far enough away from any of the buildings as not to cause any structural damage. Then he ran back to Rachel and Clay.

As he reached them the dynamite exploded, and they felt the blast. The men inside the building heard the explosion and felt the building shake. They fell silent.

Jackson pushed one of the long poles under the door and quickly withdrew it. Then he issued his ultimatum.

'Rattigan and the guard are both dead,' he said, 'and what you've just heard was a stick of dynamite exploding. We've got plenty more out here. Maybe you've noticed there's a fair gap under the barn door. We're going to push sticks of dynamite under the door tied to the end of long poles, like the one you just saw.

'They'll have short fuse-cords, and you ain't going to be able to snuff them out in time. The only way you can stop us doing this is by pushing all your hand guns and rifles under the door. You've got one minute to think about it before we push the first stick of dynamite through.'

From inside the barn, for the first thirty seconds, came the sound of agitated voices. Then the first revolver appeared from under the door, followed by another five revolvers and six rifles. This tallied with the information given by Webster that there would be six men in the barn overnight.

But if that was the case, where was Boone, whose revolver and rifle had not been in his room? Was he inside the barn?

'I want to speak to Boone,' Jackson shouted.

'He ain't here,' a voice replied from inside the barn.

'Where is he, then?' asked Jackson.

'He sleeps in the house,' the voice replied. 'If he ain't there, we don't know where he is.'

'If we find out you're lying,' shouted Jackson, 'you'll be sorry.'

But he now felt fairly sure that Boone was not in the barn, and he wondered just where he could be.

Jackson and his companions collected all the weapons from the ground outside the barn door, then settled down to await the return of Webster, who had promised to contact some volunteer townsmen who would be willing to help with the guarding of the prisoners.

When Webster reached Big Rock, he stopped the buckboard outside the hotel.

Boone, in the bedroom above the hotel entrance, stood at the window and stared down incredulously as the Webster family, clearly visible in the light from the lamp hanging outside the hotel door, climbed down from the buckboard and went inside.

Just before passing through the door, the settler glanced at the dun horse standing at the hitching rail. There was something familiar about it, but he couldn't quite place where he'd seen it before.

Boone left his room and ran to the head of the stairs leading down to the lobby. Standing there, unobserved, he heard the hotel owner, Trask, greeting the Websters. Then he heard Webster ask Trask for a room for his family.

The settler explained to Trask that a bunch of outlaws had taken over his farm for a hiding-place. Then a man called Jackson Hawke, who had been trailing the outlaws, had taken a hand. Two of the outlaws had been killed and the rest were being held in the barn.

Webster told Trask that he was returning to the farm to help Hawke and the others, but he wanted a message sending to the Ranger station at Fort Worth about the outlaws, as soon as the telegraph station opened in the morning.

'I'll attend to that,' said Trask. 'Give me the message.'

'Thanks,' said Webster, and handed it over.

'I'll take Ellen and Sally up to the room now,' said Webster, 'then I'll see if I can rustle up some men who're willing to come out tomorrow to help us guard the prisoners. Then I'll ride back to the farm.'

The shocked Boone ran back to his room, and listened as the Websters walked along the passage and into the room next door. He waited until he heard the door close, then quickly collected his things and left the hotel. Trask, who was not in the lobby, did not see him go.

Upstairs, Webster, preparing to leave, heard the door of an adjoining bedroom open and close, and the sound of footsteps along the passage outside. Moments later, glancing out through the window, he saw a big man leave the hotel. The man walked over to the dun, mounted it, and headed off down the street in a westerly direction.

Webster didn't get a view of the man's face, but as with the dun, there was something familiar about him. Intent on getting back to Jackson and the others, he dismissed the matter from his mind.

When Webster got back to the farm, Jackson told him that it looked like Boone had disappeared. The settler thought for a moment, then cursed.

'Boone rode a dun, didn't he?' he asked. Clay nodded.

'With a white stripe down its nose?' asked Webster.

'That's right,' Clay replied.

'Then I've just seen him in Big Rock,' said the settler. 'I saw him leave the hotel and ride out of town to the west. I thought there was something familiar about him, but it was dark, and as far as I knew he was still on the farm. I'm pretty sure now that it was him.

'I think he was in the room next to ours. And I think he probably saw us through the window when we drove up on the buckboard. If he stood at the top of the stairs, he'd be able to hear what I was saying to Trask.'

'Did you mention our names?' asked Jackson.

'Only yours,' Webster replied. 'I told Trask that you had trailed a bunch of outlaws to the farm. I didn't mention your two partners. And I said that two outlaws had been killed, and the rest were being held in the barn till the law picked them up.'

'I've got to get on Boone's trail as soon as I can,' said Jackson to Rachel and Clay, 'but I can't expect you two to come along, now that Rattigan's dead and Boone's on his own. It's something I can finish off myself.'

'But if *I* ain't there,' said Clay, with a rare flash of humour, 'who's going to stop you from getting lost?'

'And who,' asked Rachel, 'is going to take care of any backshooters you might run up against?'

Smiling, Jackson looked at them both for a moment before he replied.

'Thanks,' he said. 'I was scared you might take me at my word. But first, we've got to get somebody to guard these men in the barn till the Rangers pick them up.'

'That's all fixed,' said Webster. 'Three friends of mine will be riding out from town in the morning. And one of them's Brett Manning, who was a lawman in San Antonio until a year ago. Between us, I reckon we can guard these outlaws until the Rangers get here.'

The three men arrived from town two hours after sun-up, and Jackson had a few words with Manning.

'I reckon,' he said, 'that you know just as well as I do how to make sure these prisoners are still here when the Rangers arrive to pick them up.'

'Don't worry,' said Manning. 'I've guarded a lot of prisoners in my time. You can count on us handing all of these men over to the law.'

## THIRTEEN

Jackson and his two companions took their leave of Webster and the others and headed for Big Rock. On arrival there they went to see Trask and he gave them the details of Boone's brief stay. He told them that Boone had left a rifle in the hotel room, probably by mistake.

'You any idea why he wanted to see a doctor?' asked Jackson.

'No,' replied Trask. 'He didn't say why. But from the way he was acting, I got the notion that he was having pains in the belly.'

'What's the next town west of here?' asked Jackson.

'That'd be Troy,' Trask replied, 'about fifty miles along the trail. It's a bigger town than this.'

They bought some provisions at the store, then headed west. Just outside of town Clay found a hoof-print identical with one of those which they had followed from the gorge near Lasko.

'This print must have been made by Boone's horse,' he said. 'It's something for us to follow.'

Half an hour after Boone rode out of Big Rock, he realized that he had left his rifle behind. He guessed that it would only be a matter of time before Jackson Hawke was on his trail. He wondered how it was that Hawke had managed to trail him and the others all the way from the gorge near Lasko.

He had no rifle, and only enough money on him to pay a doctor's bill. Still suffering from belly pains, he tried to concentrate, as he rode along, on the details of a plan to eliminate Hawke.

He rode as fast as he was able, and arrived in Troy soon after noon. His first call was on the doctor, who diagnosed dysentery and gave him some medicine to ease the condition. Then he rode his horse along the deserted street, and round to the back of the store. Leaving his horse there, he walked round to the front.

Inside the store, the storekeeper, Herb Bailey, a frail, elderly, single man, was standing behind the counter. He eyed Boone as he came through the door, and got the impression that the stranger was a bit on edge, and in a hurry. He decided that this was not the right time to engage a customer in polite conversation.

Boone asked for a few provisions, which Bailey collected and placed in a small sack which he put on the counter. While he was doing this, Boone walked over to the window and looked out on to the street. Nothing was stirring outside. He returned to the counter and pointed to a tin of rolling tobacco on a shelf behind the storekeeper.

'I'll take one of those,' he said.

As Bailey turned to take a tin off the shelf, Boone drew his revolver and struck the storekeeper savagely over the back of the head with the barrel of his six-gun. Stunned, Bailey went down like a log, and the side of his head slammed against the top of a full keg of nails standing near the end of the counter.

Boone ran to the window, reversed the card hanging there to show CLOSED, and fastened the door from the inside. He pushed the storekeeper's body out of sight under the counter, then took all the banknotes, amounting to just over a hundred dollars, from a drawer under the counter. He walked over to a shelf on which he could see a few revolvers lying.

Lifting up a piece of sacking at the back of the shelf, he found a double-barrelled shotgun. He examined it. It appeared to be almost new, and in good working order. He placed it in a sack with some ammunition which he found on the shelf.

Then, without a glance at the motionless figure lying under the counter, he picked up the two sacks, and left the store through the living quarters at the rear of the building. Mounting his horse, and moving behind the buildings, he rode out of town unobserved, and headed west.

Jackson and his two companions, riding into Troy in the evening, some time after Boone's departure, found the town in a ferment.

It appeared that the storekeeper, a highly-respected man, had been found dead in his store, with severe head injuries, a few hours earlier. The only suspect they had was a stranger who had called in to see the doctor earlier in the day. A posse of townsmen had been formed to search for this man. Nobody had seen him leave town, and at first they had no idea which way he had gone. Then a settler rode into town from the south and told them that, a few hours earlier, he had seen a distant rider, a stranger to him, who was heading southwards. So the posse had headed off in that direction.

Jackson and his companions went to see the doctor, and explained that they were in pursuit of a man who was very likely the one who had killed the storekeeper. They asked him to describe the stranger who had called in to see him earlier in the day.

'That was him, all right,' said Jackson, when the doctor had finished. 'D'you happen to know what he took from the store?'

'There were no banknotes left in the money drawer,' replied the doctor, 'so we reckon he cleaned that out. And a man who helps out in the store sometimes said that there's a double-barrelled shotgun missing. We can't be sure whether he took anything else. Only Herb Bailey would know that.'

They thanked the doctor, then left his house and stood on the street outside.

'So, Clay,' said Jackson, 'we know that Boone's not all that far ahead of us, and he likely knows that I'm on his trail. What d'you reckon he'll do?'

'We know he has a shotgun,' Clay replied, 'and he's desperate. He's going to ambush you just as soon as he can. He's going to find a place where he can lie in wait and pick you off from cover.'

'You're probably right,' said Jackson. 'So we take extra care as we ride along after him?'

'That's right,' said Clay. 'I'm going to find out which way he was heading when he left town. You two wait here. I'll be back soon.'

He rode out of town on the trail leading west, scanning the ground as he went along, for the familiar hoof-prints of Boone's mount. After riding three-quarters of a mile, he turned and rode back to Jackson and Rachel.

'That's the way Boone went,' he said. 'Now let's find somebody around here who knows the trail west of here like the back of his hand.'

They knocked on the doctor's door, told him they were sure that Boone had ridden out of town on the trail leading west, and asked him if there was anybody in town who had a good knowledge of the trail.

'Try Jud Preston,' he said. 'He's a mule-skinner, retired now. He must have driven freight wagons along that trail hundreds of times. He lives in that shack along the street there, just past the livery stable, on the right.'

They found Preston in, and after they had introduced themselves, and explained their mission, Clay put a question to him.

'If a man were riding along that trail to the west from here.' he asked, 'and somebody was wanting to shoot him from ambush, what would the best place be for that somebody to wait?'

Preston pondered for a while before he replied.

'If I had to make a choice,' he said, 'there's one place in the next thirty miles that stands out above all the others. And it's only eleven miles from here. In fact, not all that many years ago, a lawman was ambushed and killed there by an outlaw he was chasing.

'The trail there runs between two rock outcrops, and it's barely wide enough to take a wagon through. Once when I was passing I took a good look at those outcrops. One of them has a peaked top, but the other has a flat top with a hollow in it where a man could stay out of sight. And right against this outcrop, on the south side, is a thick grove of trees.'

They thanked Preston, left his shack, and stood in the street for a while discussing their next move. Then they rode out of town, on the trail leading west. After they had covered seven miles, they camped out for the night.

They breakfasted at daybreak, then stopped, after riding along the trail for a further mile. The two outcrops described by Preston were not yet in sight.

'I'll leave you now,' said Clay. 'Watch out for me, like we planned. And let's hope we figured right about Boone waiting in ambush ahead.'

Leaving the others, Clay took a route which veered from south to west, then north, and finally approached the grove of trees which extended south from the outcrop on which they suspected Boone might be awaiting Jackson's arrival. Clay was sure that he himself would not have been spotted by anyone on the outcrop. He tethered his horse inside the grove, then walked through it towards the trail.

On his way, he came upon another horse tethered inside the grove. One glance told him that it was Boone's. He proceeded cautiously, and stood just inside the grove, near the foot of the outcrop.

When Clay had left them, Jackson and Rachel continued riding slowly along the trail and soon came in sight of the two outcrops. They stopped outside rifle range, and dismounted, then sat just off the trail, apparently resting.

Boone watched their arrival through the field-glasses which he always carried in his saddle-bag. He recognized Jackson, then turned the glasses on the woman. To his shocked surprise, he saw that it was Rachel.

Soon, he thought, they would be riding through the gap below him. At that range, a buckshot load from one barrel would probably finish them both off. But he would let them have both barrels, just to make sure.

He picked up the shotgun, checked once again that both barrels were loaded, and cocked the two triggers. Then he laid it down by his side, and continued to watch the man and the woman below.

While chatting to Rachel, Jackson kept an eye on the trees close to the foot of the outcrop. It was not long before he saw Clay briefly emerge, raise his hat twice in the air, then disappear from view.

'That means,' said Jackson, 'that Clay's found Boone's horse, and that he's going after him.'

They both rose to their feet, and gave every indication that they were preparing to continue their journey. Boone gave them his full attention.

Clay started climbing up the outcrop as silently as he could. Reaching the top, he could see Boone's shoulders and the back of his head, as the outlaw watched Rachel and Jackson walking towards their horses.

Clay got both feet on to the flat ground at the top of the slope, but, as he stood up, the ground gave way under his right foot, and he had to scramble to regain his footing. As he did so, he drew his knife. Boone heard the sound behind him, and twisted round to face Clay, reaching for the shotgun.

Clay threw his knife, and the blade thudded deep into Boone's chest just as the outlaw's finger was reaching for the trigger of the shotgun.

Boone died instantly.

Clay walked up to him and uncocked the weapon. Then he waved to Jackson and Rachel down below. They rode up to the outcrop and Jackson climbed up to join Clay.

'It's a good thing, Clay,' he said, 'that you

read the situation right. Boone could easily have killed all three of us with that shotgun.'

They carried Boone's body down to the ground and slung it over his horse. Then they all rode back to Troy. The posse had returned from a fruitless search for Boone, and they handed the body over to the leader.

They had just done this, when a party of four Texas Rangers arrived in town from the west. Ranger Tully was in charge. He told them that he was heading for the Webster farm to pick up the prisoners, and he expected a jail wagon to arrive there about the same time as they did.

They told Tully about their pursuit of Rattigan and Boone and their men. They told him that both Rattigan and Boone were now dead. He asked them to ride to Fort Worth to give evidence when the trial was held. They agreed to do this.

The trial took place two weeks later, and various sentences were imposed, including three of death by hanging.

When the trial was over, Clay told Jackson and Rachel that he intended to leave for Lasko the following morning. He said he planned to stay there a few days, then ride on to Kansas to look for a job as a lawman. Later, when they were alone, Jackson decided that it was time to discuss the future with Rachel.

'I sure am glad you came along, Rachel,' he said. 'You've been a great partner, 'specially when you stopped Red Horse from shooting me down. I'm wondering if we can make it a permanent arrangement?'

'Do I take it, Jackson Hawke,' she enquired, 'that you're asking me to marry you?'

'I guess it comes to that,' Jackson replied. 'I reckon I'd feel lost if you weren't somewhere around.'

She smiled at him.

'I've got to admit,' she said, 'that I feel the same way about you. But I'm worried about what your mother might think of the idea of having me as a daughter-in-law.'

'I know my mother, Rachel. I know her

very well. She's not going to blame you for what your stepfather did. And when she's met you, she'll be all in favour of us two getting hitched. We'll go to the Diamond H and see if she'd like us to help her run it. I'm going to send her a telegraph message right now, telling her we're on our way.'

The following morning, they set out by stage on their journey to Pueblo.

The publishers hope that this book has given you enjoyable reading. Large Print Books are especially designed to be as easy to see and hold as possible. If you wish a complete list of our books please ask at your local library or write directly to:

**Dales Large Print Books**
Magna House, Long Preston,
Skipton, North Yorkshire.
BD23 4ND

This Large Print Book, for people
who cannot read normal print,
is published under the auspices of
**THE ULVERSCROFT FOUNDATION**

... we hope you have enjoyed this book.
Please think for a moment about those
who have worse eyesight than you ...
and are unable to even read or enjoy
Large Print without great difficulty.

You can help them by sending a
donation, large or small, to:

**The Ulverscroft Foundation,
1, The Green, Bradgate Road,
Anstey, Leicestershire, LE7 7FU,
England.**
or request a copy of our brochure for
more details.

The Foundation will use all donations
to assist those people who are visually
impaired and need special attention
with medical research, diagnosis
and treatment.

Thank you very much for your help.